No Witnesses

"Everybody just take it easy!" Clint called.

They all turned and stared. Gunner was the only one on his feet, and he did what his gut told him to do. He went for his gun.

Clint drew and fired. The bullet hit Gunner in the midsection and folded him up.

Cain fired, too, and despite what he'd told Clint, his first bullet hit Gunner.

The others, realizing they were in a cross fire, reacted badly. They all jumped to their feet, going for their guns.

"Damn it!" Clint swore. As the four men leveled their guns to fire, he doubted he and Cain would be able to keep any of them alive.

He was right.

DON'T MISS THESE
ALL-ACTION WESTERN SERIES
FROM THE BERKLEY PUBLISHING GROUP

THE GUNSMITH by J. R. Roberts
Clint Adams was a legend among lawmen, outlaws, and ladies.
They called him . . . the Gunsmith.

LONGARM by Tabor Evans
The popular long-running series about Deputy U.S. Marshal
Custis Long—his life, his loves, his fight for justice.

SLOCUM by Jake Logan
Today's longest-running action Western. John Slocum rides a
deadly trail of hot blood and cold steel.

BUSHWHACKERS by B. J. Lanagan
An action-packed series by the creators of Longarm! The rousing
adventures of the most brutal gang of cutthroats ever assembled—
Quantrill's Raiders.

DIAMONDBACK by Guy Brewer
Dex Yancey is Diamondback, a Southern gentleman turned con
man when his brother cheats him out of the family fortune.
Ladies love him. Gamblers hate him. But nobody pulls one over
on Dex . . .

WILDGUN by Jack Hanson
The blazing adventures of mountain man Will Barlow—from
the creators of Longarm!

TEXAS TRACKER by Tom Calhoun
J.T. Law: the most relentless—and dangerous—manhunter in
all Texas. Where sheriffs and posses fail, he's the best man to
bring in the most vicious outlaws—for a price.

THE GUNSMITH

386

VENGEANCE RIDE

J. R. ROBERTS

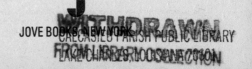

JOVE BOOKS, NEW YORK

THE BERKLEY PUBLISHING GROUP
Published by the Penguin Group
Penguin Group (USA) LLC
375 Hudson Street, New York, New York 10014

USA • Canada • UK • Ireland • Australia • New Zealand • India • South Africa • China

penguin.com

A Penguin Random House Company

VENGEANCE RIDE

A Jove Book / published by arrangement with the author

Copyright © 2014 by Robert J. Randisi.

For information, address: The Berkley Publishing Group,
a division of Penguin Group (USA),
375 Hudson Street, New York, New York 10014.

ISBN: 978-0-515-15443-6

PUBLISHING HISTORY
Jove mass-market edition / February 2014

PRINTED IN THE UNITED STATES OF AMERICA

10 9 8 7 6 5 4 3 2 1

Cover illustration by Sergio Giovine.

ONE

Clint Adams always hated when somebody tried to shoot him from an ambush, and this time was no exception.

For a man with a reputation, this was not as rare an occurrence as he might wish. Although he hadn't counted, he felt that he was launching himself out of his saddle for the hundredth time. One of these days he was likely to land on his head and kill himself that way.

He landed as well as he could, although it was always bone-jarring. Rolling on impact was meant to minimize that impact, but he wasn't sure it worked all that well. His teeth rattled and his bones threatened to crack as he landed, rolled, and came up with his Colt in his hand.

Lead bit into the dirt around him, and he quickly looked around for cover.

Eclipse, his Darley Arabian, had been through this almost as much as he had. The horse did the right thing, galloped off far enough to be out of the way of flying lead, but not so far that Clint wouldn't be able to collect him when it was all over.

As Clint ran for cover to a copse of trees, he realized the lead was coming at him from more than one direction. He took cover, ducked low, and waited while they got tired of shooting at the trees. This time helped him to hear the different guns that were firing. He counted three.

The shooting stopped. Nobody called out to him, but he was sure they knew where he was. They could have been moving in on him, getting closer by the second. He had to move.

He worked his way through the trees to come out the other side. If he had been with three men, trying to kill one, and he knew the one was in among the trees, he would have left a man to cover the three. As he came out, nobody fired at him. Apparently, all three were moving in on him.

They knew enough to keep quiet while they were doing it. But they allowed him to slip out the back, find new cover. They were used to working together, but they were not used to doing this.

He found his way to a ravine, slid down into it, and waited, listening. They were bound to talk to one another sooner or later.

He remained still, gun in hand, listening . . .

"Where'd he go?" Derrick Sands asked.

"Quiet!" Adam Dunn snapped.

"What's the difference?" Sands asked. "He's out here, he's on foot. What's the difference if he hears us?"

"He went into those trees," Larry Allen said. "I saw him."

"Then he's still in there," Sands said.

"No."

They both turned and looked at Dunn.

"Whataya mean?"

"I mean we made a mistake," Dunn said.

"What mistake?" Sands asked.

"Other than we missed," Allen added.

"One of us should have stayed up on the ridge, watching. We could have seen if he came out of the trees. Now we don't know for sure."

"Well," Sands said, "I'm goin' in after him."

"Larry, you cover him."

"What are you gonna do?"

"Wait out there," Dunn said, "in case he comes out when you go in."

"He ain't comin' out of there," Sands said. "Not alive anyway."

"Well, go ahead, then," Dunn said.

As the other two moved in on the copse of trees, Dunn backed away. He and his partners were new to this manhunting game, but he never should have made that mistake.

The Gunsmith was out there, somewhere.

Clint turned over onto his belly, peered up out of the ravine. He could see the trees from there, kept his gun ready. If they went in there, they'd have to come out. If they didn't come out the same way they went in, he'd have them.

Dunn looked off in the near distance, saw the Gunsmith's horse standing there. Could the animal be that well trained? He wondered what it would do if he walked to it.

He had taken his eyes off Sands and Allen to look at the horse. When he looked back, they were gone, having entered the thicket of trees.

Sands poked in among the trees with his rifle barrel. Allen came up behind him.

"Nothin'," Sands said. "He ain't in here."

"Then where is he?" Allen asked.

"He musta gone all the way through."

"I'll check," Allen said, and strode past Sands, who shouted, "Wait!"

Too late.

TWO

As the man stepped out from the trees, Clint fired. He had no qualms about doing it. The man was holding his rifle like he intended to use it. The bullet struck him in the chest, dropping him so that he fell back into the trees. His rifle slipped from his hands, and lay just outside the tree line.

Clint waited to see what would happen next . . .

Sands saw Allen stagger as the bullet struck him, and then fall.

"Damn it!" he snapped.

He turned to run back out of the trees the other way.

Dunn heard the shot, just one, wondered what it meant. He watched the trees, waiting for his men to come back out, but only Sands did.

"What happened?" Dunn demanded.

"Adams got Larry," Sands said.

"Damn it," Dunn said. "We lost our advantage. Let's get out of here."

"There's still two of us," Sands said. "We can still take 'im."

"He's the Gunsmith, and he knows we're here," Dunn

said. "We need to get out of here, regroup, get some more help, and try again."

"What about his horse?"

They both looked over at the big Darley Arabian, standing calmly.

"Kill it," Dunn said.

Sands raised his rifle, but just as he fired, the horse moved. He tried to get it with a second shot, but the animal wouldn't stand still.

"Forget it!" Dunn told him. "Let's just get the hell out of here before he comes lookin' for us."

Sands, ten years younger than the forty-year-old Dunn, asked, "Are you afraid of him?"

"You bet I am!" Dunn said. "If you're smart, you'll be scared, too."

Dunn turned and ran back toward their own horses. Reluctantly, Sands followed him.

Clint waited a little longer. He thought he heard voices, but he didn't see anyone for the next few minutes. He also couldn't see Eclipse, but he suddenly heard two shots and they weren't directed at him.

He broke his cover, left the ravine, and ran to the fallen man's rifle. Picking it up, he circled around the stand of trees rather than going through again.

As he came around the trees, he saw Eclipse standing off in the near distance, but rather than standing calmly, the horse seemed agitated. He continued around until he came to the point where he had first been shot at. There was nobody around, and nobody took a shot at him. Apparently, the other men decided to run when they lost their advantage.

He walked to Eclipse and grabbed his reins.

"Easy, big fella," he said. He checked the big horse, found a wound on his neck where a bullet had grazed him. It had happened either during the original ambush, or as a result of the two shots Clint had heard later. They'd tried to shoot

Eclipse in order to leave Clint on foot. That made Clint even angrier than being shot at himself.

He held the reins tightly and walked the horse back to where he'd left the fallen man. He put the rifle down, grabbed the dead man's boots, and pulled him from the trees. He then went through his pockets, but found nothing. He looked at the man's face. Fairly young, probably in his thirties, but it was not a face that Clint recognized.

The town he'd left behind him was Wells, Arizona. These three had probably spotted him there and decided to come after him. Normally, he would have taken the dead man back there with him to try and have him identified. But Eclipse had a wound, and he wasn't going to ride the Darley himself, so he certainly wasn't going to throw the dead man over his saddle.

No, his only play was to continue on to the next town. He'd seen a signpost about a mile back that said he was approaching a town called Hastings. He decided to walk Eclipse there, have the wound treated, and then talk to the law there to see what he could find out about three men riding together.

He took the man by the boots again, and this time dragged him deeper into the trees. Maybe that would keep him safe from varmints until somebody could come out and pick him up. He also dropped the dead man's rifle next to him.

He checked Eclipse's neck again. The wound was bleeding, and while the animal stood calmly while he examined him, he knew it hurt. He used a dirty shirt from his saddlebags to try to stanch the flow of blood. He hoped he'd come to a water hole or stream between here and town so he could wash the wound out.

"Okay, big guy, let's go," he said, grabbing the reins. "We'll walk at your pace and get you some help." They started walking together.

THREE

Clint did find a stream on his way to Hastings, so was able to wash out the wound on Eclipse's neck. But his first stop in town would still be a vet—if the town had one.

He walked Eclipse down the main street, the walk having taken them a couple of hours. People turned to look at the dusty man walking the big Darley Arabian horse.

"Excuse me," Clint called out to a man.

"Yeah?"

"Has this town got a vet?"

"Yeah, that'd be Doc Martin."

"Where can I find him?"

"Walk down about another two blocks. When you pass the Jack of Hearts Saloon, it'll be on the corner."

"Thanks."

Clint passed the saloon and saw the vet's shingle hanging in front of the corner building. He left Eclipse standing in front and knocked on the door. It was opened by a handsome woman in her thirties. "Can I help you?" she asked.

"Yes, I'm looking for the vet, Doc Martin?"

"I'm afraid he's not here," she said. "He was called away on an emergency early this morning. He hasn't returned yet."

"Oh," Clint said, "well—"

The woman looked past him, and her pretty violet eyes widened.

"Is that your horse?"

"Yes, it is."

"He's magnificent. What's wrong with him? I mean, I assume you're here for him?"

"Yes, ma'am," Clint said. "He was shot."

"Shot? Who would shoot such an animal?"

"Well, I'm afraid they were trying to shoot me."

That fact didn't seem to upset her as much.

She stepped out the door and approached Eclipse. He shied from her, but she spoke to him soothingly and he decided to stand calmly and allow her to examine him.

"I can handle this," she told Clint. "Bring him around to the side of the building, please. I'll meet you there."

"Yes, ma'am," Clint said. "Thank you."

She went back inside, but was waiting at a side door as he walked Eclipse around the corner.

"Walk him right in," she instructed.

He did as she asked, found himself in an enclosed area that was used to examine and treat large animals.

"I can clean this wound and disinfect it," she said. "You can go and talk to the sheriff about being shot at."

"Yes, ma'am," he said, "I'll do that. Um, are you . . . Mrs. Martin?"

"Miss," she said. "The doctor is my father."

"My name is Clint," he said.

"And what is this handsome gent's name?" she asked.

"Eclipse."

"Well, Eclipse," she said, stroking him, "I think you and I are going to get along just fine." She turned her head and seemed surprised that Clint was still there. "The sheriff's office is just up the street. His name is Ingram. He's not very good at his job, but he's all we've got."

"I see," Clint said. "Well, I'll go and talk to him and then come on back."

"I should be done by then," she assured him.

"Thank you, Miss Martin."

He left the vet's, closing the door behind him, and headed for the sheriff's office.

As Clint approached the sheriff's office, the door opened and a man wearing a badge stepped out. He turned and walked directly toward Clint. He was a tall, handsome man who wore his hat at a jaunty angle, and wore a dark blue bandanna around his neck. The care he seemed to take with his appearance extended to his badge, which had a high shine on it.

"Excuse me, Sheriff."

The man stopped short and looked Clint over.

"Yes?"

"My name's Clint Adams. I need to talk—"

"Adams? The Gunsmith?"

"That's right."

"What brings you to my town, Mr. Adams?"

"Well, three men tried to ambush me a few miles out. They managed to wound my horse."

"Not you?"

"No," Clint said, "I managed to escape with a few bumps and bruises."

"And your horse?"

"I left him with the vet."

"Doc Martin got called away this mornin'."

"I know," Clint said. "His daughter is treating the wound."

"Andrea," Ingram said. "She's capable. Well, come into my office and I'll take a report."

"You looked like you were on your way somewhere," Clint said.

"That's okay," Ingram said. "I want to hear your story. And in the office, I can offer you some coffee."

"Sounds good to me," Clint said, following the man back to his office.

FOUR

The office reflected the man, in that it was very clean. So were the coffee mugs the sheriff filled. He handed one to Clint and then sat behind his desk. There was nothing on top of it but a pencil.

"Tell me what happened," he said.

Clint described the encounter to the lawman, who listened without interruption. Ingram was in his forties, seemed—in the short time Clint had known him, of course—to be competent enough. He wondered what Andrea Martin had against the man.

"Well," Ingram said when Clint was done, "I guess the thing to do is send a telegram to the sheriff in Wells with a description of these men. I'll also pass the description around town, and give it to my deputies."

"How many deputies do you have?"

"Two," Ingram said, "young men I'm showin' the ropes to. They'll be good lawmen with some experience."

"Well, I just want you to know I'll be keeping my eyes out for those men while I'm here."

"And how long do you think that'll be, Mr. Adams?"

"I don't know," Clint said. "I guess the vet will tell me that."

"I hope if you see the two men," Ingram said, "you'll let me know, instead of bracing them yourself."

"I guess we'll have to see about that, Sheriff," Clint said. "It'll depend on the circumstances."

"Fair enough."

Clint put his coffee mug down on the desk and stood up.

"Got a suggestion for a hotel?" he asked.

"We got two, and there's not much difference between them," Ingram said. "Clean beds."

"Okay, thanks. Will you let me know when you've sent that telegram?"

"Sure will."

"I'm going to go and check on my horse before I get a hotel room."

"I'll find you," Ingram promised.

Clint nodded his thanks and left the office.

When he got back to the vet's, he started to walk to the front door, then decided to go around to the side instead. There was a window on the door, and he could see Andrea Martin inside, tending to Eclipse, who was standing calmly and—it seemed to Clint—leaning into her touch.

He knocked on the door.

Her head jerked in surprise, her eyes wide, then she saw him and relaxed. She walked to the door and unlocked it.

"Sorry if I startled you," Clint said.

"That's okay," she said. "I was concentrating on your horse."

"How's he doing?"

"The wound wasn't bad," she said. "I'm glad you were careful, though, and walked him into town."

"I'd never take chances with him," Clint assured her.

She walked back to the horse and he followed. She'd obviously applied a poltice to the wound, packing it tightly.

"We'll leave that on until tomorrow and then have a look," she said.

"Suits me," Clint said. "I'll be in town for a while anyway. I've got some business to attend to."

"Finding the men who tried to kill you?"

"Exactly."

"Was the sheriff any help?"

"He was, actually."

"Hmm," was all she said.

"How long has he been sheriff here?"

"About two years," she said. "He's serving his second term."

"What have you got against him?"

"That story is too long," she said, "and I don't know you well enough to tell you."

"Well, maybe you could get to know me better if you accompanied me to supper tonight?"

"I don't think so," she said. "I have to stay here until my father comes back. But thank you for the offer."

She struck him as the type of woman who'd had some problems with men, maybe even been hurt—maybe recently by Sheriff Ingram, who was a handsome man.

"Well," he said, touching Eclipse's nose, "I'll go and get myself a hotel room, and then something to eat."

"Try the Harvest House Hotel," she said.

"The sheriff said there wasn't much difference between the hotels."

"Hmm," she said again, "well, the Harvest House has a very good dining room."

"Thanks for the tip," he said. "I'll be able to kill two birds with one stone."

"Come by in the morning," she said. "My father should be back by then, and he'll take a look at Eclipse just to be sure I didn't miss anything."

"I doubt you did," he said, "but I appreciate the care."

She let him out, said good night, and locked the door behind him.

FIVE

Clint checked into the Harvest House Hotel, found the room clean, the bed adequate. He left his saddlebags and rifle in the room and went down to the dining room.

His steak and vegetables were well cooked, and the coffee was to his liking. Andrea Martin had steered him to the right hotel.

He was starting in on a slice of apple pie when the sheriff appeared.

"Have a seat, Sherriff," Clint said. "Coffee?"

"Don't mind if I do," the lawman said. He sat and poured a cup. "This hotel suit you?"

"It's fine," Clint said. "Actually, it was Miss Martin who sent me over here."

"Ah," Ingram said. "I don't suppose she had anything good to say about me."

"As a matter of fact, no."

Ingram winced.

"She say anything bad?"

"Not really," Clint said. "Didn't have much to say, actually. But I get the feeling there's . . . history there."

"There is, but that's not important," he said. "I sent that

telegram to the sheriff in Wells, and got a reply pretty quick. I also sent my deputies out to pick up that body."

"Anything helpful from the sheriff?"

"Not yet," he said. "He's gonna check around, see what he can find out. If the three men spotted you in town and recognized you, they might have talked about planning to ambush you."

"And no word on a couple of strangers riding in here recently?"

"No," Ingram said, shaking his head. He was holding the coffee cup in front of him, talking over it, taking small sips in between. "I'm still checking, though. I can let you know when we have the body at the undertaker's."

"Good," Clint said. "I'd like to take another look at it. Maybe it'll look familiar when I can study him without having to worry about being shot in the back."

Ingram finished his coffee and set the cup down, pushed his chair back.

"Well, I better get to it, then," he said. "I'll send word when the body comes in."

"Appreciate it, Sheriff."

"Sure thing," Ingram said. "I don't like the idea of somebody being ambushed in my county."

"Believe me," Clint said, "neither do I."

Clint finished his pie and coffee and left the hotel. An idea had occurred to him while he was eating, and he decided to act on it. He walked through town, found the people pleasant enough as they nodded to him in passing, even though he was a stranger.

Eventually he came to the storefront he was looking for—the telegraph office. He went inside and sent two telegrams of his own. One went to his friend Rick Hartman in Labyrinth, Texas, and the other went to Talbot Roper in Denver. Roper was a private detective—probably the best in the country—and a good friend.

Both telegrams asked the same question. Had either man

heard any news about a price being put on Clint's head? Of
course, the three men might have simply spotted him in
Wells and decided to try and make a name for themselves,
but there were also a lot of people out there with money who
would like to see the Gunsmith dead. There was no harm
in checking that out.

He told the clerk he was staying at the Harvest House,
and asked that any replies be brought there.

He left the office, stopped just outside. The sheriff didn't
know anything about two strangers riding into town together
recently, but what if they had decided to ride in separately?

There were three people who either kept track of strangers in town, or they were simply in a position to have that
information. They were the local lawman, bartenders, and
men who owned or worked in livery stables.

Clint had already talked with the sheriff, so that left
saloons and livery stables.

He decided to try the saloons first.

SIX

There were four saloons in Hastings. Two were holes in the wall, real small, with no girls or gambling. Clint nursed a beer in each of them. First he listened to the conversation around him. He could often pick out strangers that way. However, the few patrons in each of these saloons seemed to know each other very well. In the end, he asked the bartenders if they'd seen any strangers in town, and they each had the same answer:

"Just you."

The other two saloons were larger, with all the trappings: girls, gambling, music.

He stopped at the Wild Horse Saloon first, decided to save the Jack of Hearts for last.

The Wild Horse was crowded for midday, girls already working the floor, gaming tables already open and in full swing. Clint made room for himself at the bar and ordered a beer. Unlike the beer at the other two saloons, this one was ice cold.

He followed the same sequence, first waiting and listening. While this saloon was crowded, most of the customers seemed to know one another, and the bartender.

"I'm looking for two strangers," he said to the mean-looking barman. "They may have come in together, or separately."

"What did they do?" The barman rubbed a big hand over his black stubbles.

"They tried to ambush me," Clint said. "Backshoot me."

"Why?"

"That's what I'm going to ask them when I see them," Clint said.

"Well," the man said, "I ain't seen 'em, apart or together."

"So you know everybody in here right now?" Clint asked him.

The bartender took a toothpick from his mouth and said, "Everybody but you."

Clint finished his beer and left.

He stopped into the Jack of Hearts, down the street from the vet's. He ordered a beer, listened, then questioned the bartender, who looked like the other one's brother, right down to the stubble and the toothpick.

"Two men?" the bartender asked.

"There were three when they tried to kill me," Clint said. "Now there's two."

"Ain't seen 'em," the man said.

"You seen any strangers yesterday or today?" Clint asked.

"Only you."

"Have you got a brother?"

The man stared at him.

"Yeah, why?"

"I think I just met him a while ago."

"And what did he say?"

"Same thing."

"Exactly?"

"Exactly."

The man grinned.

"That was my brother, all right."

"You guys aren't very helpful."

"Maybe," the bartender said, "if we saw somethin', we'd tell you."

"Maybe," Clint said, "I'll ask again sometime."

"Another beer?"

"No, thanks," Clint said.

"Come back sometime," the bartender said.

"Oh, I will."

Clint left the saloon. His intentions were to check the livery stables, but as he left the saloon, he saw Andrea Martin leaving the vet's office.

He intercepted her before she could get very far. She started when she saw him, drawing back a foot.

"I'm sorry," he said. "It seems I'm always startling you."

"Oh, Mr. Adams," she said. "Were you coming to check on your horse again?"

"No, actually I was coming out of the saloon when I saw you walking here."

"And?"

"And I thought maybe I could walk you to wherever you were going."

"Why?"

He was taken aback by the question.

"To be neighborly."

"But we're not neighbors."

"Well then . . . to look after you. A lady shouldn't walk alone, especially when it's getting dark."

"It's hardly dusk," she said, "and this is my town. I have nothing to fear."

"I'm starting to think you just don't want my company," he said.

"Mr. Adams," she said, "you're passing through town. You're a good-looking man. I'm sure you've been on the trail a long time and you're looking for a girl. I'm not that girl. But there are plenty of them in the saloon."

Clint stared at her, no words coming to mind.

Suddenly she frowned.

"I've offended you."

"Well . . ."

She put her hands over her mouth.

"Is it possible—" she started.

"You misjudged me?"

She nodded.

"If I have, I'm sorry. It's just that a lot of men come through town looking for girls."

"I see."

"If you're not that kind of man, I'm sorry."

"I see. And if I am?"

"Now you're making fun of me."

"Well, I won't do that anymore," he said. "I'll be on my way, and you can go and . . . do whatever it is you were going to do."

"I was going to get something to eat," she said. "Normally I would cook for my father and myself, but since he's not back yet, I was just going to get a bite."

"Well, go ahead," he said. "I won't stop you."

"Maybe I can—"

"I'll see you in the morning," he said. "Maybe your father will be back, and you won't even have to talk to me again."

"That's not fai—"

He cut her off by turning and walking away, a slight smile on his face.

SEVEN

Clint went back to the Jack of Hearts later that night, had a few beers, watched the activity going on. Every so often he looked at the bartender—whose name was Mack—and he'd shake his head. No strangers.

There were poker and faro tables, but nothing else. The seats were all taken, but even when one opened up, Clint was not interested in playing.

There was something—rather, someone—who was attracting his interest, though. Her name was Maria, a Mexican with a lovely Spanish accent. She worked the saloon floor very gracefully, managing to avoid most of the groping male hands and laughing about it. When she laughed, her eyes flashed. Every so often she tossed her head to get her black hair out of her eyes. And during the course of the night, she kept finding reasons to come over to where Clint was standing at the bar.

One time she said, "I hear you're lookin' for some strangers."

"A couple," he said "See any?"

"Only you."

"That's what I keep hearing."

"Well, my name's Maria. I'll keep my eyes peeled."

"Thanks."

Later she came back with an empty tray and set it on the bar for the bartender to fill with drinks.

"Not interested in gamblin'?" she asked him.

"Not tonight."

"Maybe you'd just like to talk?" she asked.

"That would be nice."

"Yeah, well, I noticed you haven't been talkin' to any of the men around you, so I thought maybe . . . a woman?"

"Do you have anyone in mind?"

She smiled, picked up her tray, and said, "I'll let you know."

As it got later, she stopped by him more often, and they did talk. She'd been living in Hastings for five years, had bought herself a small house outside town. She admitted to him that she used to work as a whore, but for the past few years she'd only been working as a saloon girl. No men. At least, not for money.

"Only when it's somebody I like," she said. "Or somebody who intrigues me."

"And which am I?"

"A little of both, I suppose," she said.

And in the end, when her shift was over, she took him home with her, with the promise of a bath . . . and a lot more . . .

She drew a bath for him, told him she'd give him some privacy. Alone in the room, he stripped, set his gun on a chair by the tub, and lowered himself into the hot water.

He lay back in the bathtub, enjoying how the steaming water soothed his aching muscles. After the day he'd had, it did him no end of good to just relax and have some peace and quiet. His arms hung over the sides of the tub. When he shifted one hand, his fingers bumped against something that was warm, soft, and hadn't been there before. He sat bolt upright and turned to find Maria circling around the tub.

She wasn't wearing a stitch of clothing, and his fingers had brushed against the smooth, dark skin of her leg.

"I surprise you?" she asked in her sultry Spanish accent.

"Maybe a little," Clint replied.

She glanced toward the nearby chair, where his holster hung along with his hat. "You want to get to your gun?"

"Do I need it?"

She smiled and climbed in with him. Sitting with her back against the opposite end of the tub from Clint, Maria nestled against the curved metal. When she rested her arms along the edge, water splashed against her breasts, causing her large, dark nipples to harden. "You don't need that gun," she said with a smile. Her foot moved beneath the water to slip between Clint's legs. "But I think you might need this one."

Clint was surprised she could fit inside that tub with him. He was surprised again when she found the room to move forward as if to sit on his lap. He met her halfway by scooting forward until she was able to straddle him properly. Her hands slid along the edge of the tub until they met behind his head. Maria looked down at him and smiled expectantly with her full, deep red lips.

"I can feel your gun now, *señor*," she said while grinding against his growing erection.

"You'll feel it even better in a minute." With that, Clint wrapped his arms around her and pulled her closer. Maria's fingers slid through his hair as she arched her back and her entire body trembled when he started teasing her nipples with his tongue.

Her body was taut and muscular. Her skin smelled of perspiration, smoke . . . and yet a heady, sensual smell, as well. When Clint touched her, she responded out of pure instinct, twisting and turning to guide his tongue where she wanted it to go while shifting her weight until his hard cock brushed against the right spot between her thighs.

Clint licked one breast and then the other before running his tongue straight up between them to taste her neck. She was salty. The bath would take care of that.

He kept one hand upon her rounded hip while reaching down with the other to guide his rigid pole into her warm pussy. As soon as he entered her, Clint pumped up to drive every inch of his cock into her tight embrace. Maria gripped the edges of the tub with both hands, leaning back until her long dark hair touched the water behind her.

With both hands on her hips again, Clint held her in place as he drove into her again and again. With a bit of gentle encouragement, he got her to lift herself up just a bit so he could plunge into her at a better angle. When he buried even more of his cock into her, she opened her eyes wide and pulled in a sharp breath. Maria's smile widened and she exhaled slowly amid a long string of whispered Spanish words. Before long, she took the reins by leaning forward and holding on to the tub near Clint's shoulders. Her body writhed slowly back and forth, riding his shaft while continuing to whisper into his ear.

Clint ran his hands up and down along her back while kissing her breasts and neck. He found a sweet spot that got her moving faster as he licked it, and when he tested her with a few gentle bites, Maria's entire body tensed. She stopped moving, which prompted him to start thrusting again. This time, he moved with shorter, more powerful strokes. Maria responded by looking him straight in the eyes and grabbing the back of his head with one hand.

They remained locked that way for the next several minutes. She watched him with eyes that told him everything he needed to know. As soon as she wanted more, he gave it to her. When she was ready to be pushed over the edge, he grabbed her hips in both hands and took her there.

Maria sat up straight and bounced up and down as Clint pounded into her. Her back became rigid and she held on to the sides of the tub for support while opening her legs as far as she could. Water splashed over their bodies and onto the floor. Her breasts swayed to the rhythm of their movements, and her voice became strained until it caught in the back of her throat. Clint waited for a second until she caught her breath. Then he drove up into her again, burying every inch of his rigid pole between her legs. Maria leaned back and let out a shuddering cry until her climax rolled through her entire body like a storm. When she opened her eyes again, she smiled and started riding him with renewed vigor.

Clint leaned back as she bounced on top of him. Maria knew exactly how to shift her body and when to pump her hips to drive him out of his mind. Finally, she took every inch of him inside her and rocked back and forth until he was past the point of no return.

EIGHT

The next morning Clint slipped out of Maria's house without waking her. He walked back to his hotel and had breakfast there, then went over to the vet's office. This time he went to the front door again, and when he knocked, it was opened by an older man.

"Dr. Martin?" he asked.

"Doc Martin is fine," the man said. "I'm a vet, not a doctor. You must be Mr. Adams."

"That's right."

The two men shook hands.

"Come on in," Martin said.

Clint entered, and Martin closed the door and turned to face him.

"That's a mighty fine animal you got there," the man said. He was tall, probably seventy or so, so there was a slight stoop that took away some of the height he used to have.

"Yeah, thanks," Clint said. "He's kind of special."

"Well, I'll take you see to him," Martin said. "I gotta tell you, Andrea took real good care of him while I was away."

Clint followed the vet through to the room he used for large animals, where Eclipse was standing calmly. There was no sign of Andrea.

"There he is," Martin said. "Like I said, my daughter did a fine job with him, and he's gonna heal just fine."

"How long?"

"A few days, I'd think. I guess you can find something to do in town until then. I understand you're lookin' for the men who shot at you and hit your horse."

"That's right," Clint said.

"You intend to kill them?"

Clint decided to be honest.

"If all they had done was shoot at me, maybe not," Clint said, "but they shot my horse."

"Believe me," he said, "I understand that. Especially an animal like this one."

"Tell me what I owe you—" Clint started.

"We can take care of that later," the doctor said. "We still have some time."

"I'm sorry your daughter's not here," Clint said. "I'd like to thank her."

"I'm sure you'll see her again when you come to pick your horse up," Martin said. "Here, I'll let you out this way."

Martin opened the side door to let Clint out and said, "Come by anytime."

"I will. Thanks."

Clint was coming back around the corner when he saw the sheriff coming the other way.

"I stopped at your hotel and they told me you just left," Ingram said. "We've got the body over at the undertaker's."

"Good," Clint said. "Let's go over and take a look."

Ingram led the way.

NINE

When they got to the undertaker's, Ingram took Clint right in to see the body. The undertaker himself wasn't around.

"Do you know him?" Clint asked.

"Never saw him before."

Clint took a look at the face again. He had the same reaction as he'd had out on the trail—nothing. He didn't know the man, didn't think he'd ever seen him before.

"Find anything on him?"

"Nothin'."

That fit with what Clint knew. He'd gone through the man's pockets and had come up empty.

"What about a horse?" Clint asked.

"Didn't find one. It either ran off, or his partners took it with them."

"What about a trail left by the other two?" Clint asked.

"I've got my best trackers out there lookin'," Ingram said. "If they left a trail, we'll find it."

Clint took a last look at the body. The clothes were trail worn, as was the gun. This was a man who was not used to having money, so he'd probably taken the job for that reason rather than something personal.

Clint had just killed a young man named Travis, who had

something personal against him, but took months to reveal himself. This man had clearly done what he did for money. The question was, what about the other two? Maybe one of them had a personal grudge and had hired the other two to back his play.

"Seen enough?" Ingram asked.

Clint shook his head and said, "I've seen nothing. There's nothing helpful here, so yeah, I guess I'm done."

"Come on," Ingram said, "let's get a drink."

They left the undertaker's office and walked to one of the smaller saloons. When they entered, the only person there was the bartender.

"Leo, beers for me and my friend."

"Comin' up, Sheriff," the bartender said.

He set two beers on the bar. Ingram picked one up and handed it to Clint.

"What are your plans now?" he asked.

"My horse needs a few days, so I'll be around waiting to see what your trackers come up with."

Ingram raised his beer mug and said, "Maybe you can even relax."

"I doubt that," Clint said. "I've sent out some telegrams to see if I can pick up some information."

"You think maybe somebody out there is after you?" Ingram asked. "Spending some money?"

"Maybe."

"Well," Ingram said, "I hope we can come up with the answers for you." He drank half his beer and set the mug down on the bar. "I've got to get back to work. I'll see you later."

"Thanks for your help, Sheriff."

"Just doin' my job, Mr. Adams," Ingram said.

"Thanks anyway."

Ingram nodded and left the saloon. Clint looked at the bartender, who was cleaning a glass and watching him.

"What's on your mind?" Clint asked.

The man shrugged.

"I was just listenin'."

"And?"

"I may have somethin' for you."

"Like what?"

"Information."

"And what's it going to cost me?"

"A few bucks."

"It will have to be worth it."

"There was a stranger in here last night."

"Just one?"

"Just one, but he talked about a partner."

Clint didn't think he had enough money in his pocket to make the man talk further. He could have shaken it out of him—or scared it out—but he decided not to.

"Okay," Clint said. "I'll be back for the information."

"Don't you wanna know how much I want?"

"I'm going to come back with some money," Clint said. "With however much I feel the information is worth." He put down his beer mug. "And you're going to take it."

He turned and walked out, headed for the bank.

TEN

Clint needed to send a telegram before he could go to the bank. He also needed to get a reply.

"I'll be at the café across the street when the reply comes in," Clint told the telegraph operator.

"Yes, sir."

"Any replies from my other telegrams?"

"Well, yes, sir," the young clerk said. "I took them to your hotel, like you said. Left them with the desk clerk. You wasn't there."

"No, I wasn't," Clint said. "Okay, I'll be across the street."

"Yes, sir."

Clint walked out, crossed the street, and entered the café. It was between breakfast and lunch, so he had his pick of any table. He chose one against the back wall. Just once he'd like to sit at the window and look out while he ate, but the Gunsmith in a window was just too much of a target.

"Sir?" the waiter asked.

"Coffee, and pie," Clint said.

"Apple, rhubarb, or peach."

"Peach," Clint said.

"Comin' up, sir."

He was waiting for his pie when Andrea Martin entered

the café. She walked directly to him. She was wearing a simple cotton dress and boots, carrying a drawstring bag.

"Hello, Miss Martin."

"Mr. Adams," she said. "May I sit down?"

"Of course," he said. "Coffee?"

"Please."

He signaled the waiter to bring two cups when he brought the pot. The man nodded.

"Is this a coincidence?" he asked.

"No, it is not," she said. "I saw you come in here."

"I saw your father this morning."

"I know." She lowered her eyes. "I was in another room when you came. I was . . . avoiding you."

"That makes it odd that you'd come in here looking for me," he said.

"Yes, I know," she said. "I was . . . ashamed, so I came to apologize."

"For what exactly?"

Before she could answer, the waiter came with the coffee and pie.

"Anything else for Miss Martin?" the waiter asked.

"No, nothing," she said. "Thank you."

He nodded and withdrew.

"Go ahead," she said. "Eat your pie."

"Will you answer my question?"

She sat back in her chair, took a deep breath.

"I apparently misjudged you yesterday," she said. "I'm sorry for that. I suppose . . . you're not like other men."

"I'd like to believe that," Clint said.

"I'm also sorry I avoided you this morning," she said. "That was . . . silly."

"It's okay," he said. "I forgive you."

"For which time?"

"Either," Clint said, "both. Take your pick. I don't hold a grudge."

"Not even against the men who shot your horse?"

"Well," he said, "them . . . that's different. No, I don't hold a grudge against you."

"I hope not," she said.

"Your father said you did a fine job on Eclipse."

"The horse wasn't really hurt that bad," she said. "Be good as new in a few days."

"Good."

She took one sip of coffee, then put the cup down and stood up.

"I have to go and pick up a few things for my dad," she said.

"Can I walk you?" he asked. "This time?"

She studied him a moment, then said, "Sure, why not?"

"Finish your coffee," he said. "I'll finish my pie, and then we'll go."

She sat back down.

Before he'd finished his pie, the clerk from the telegraph office appeared in the doorway.

"Got your answer, sir," he said, handing Clint the telegram.

"Thanks." Clint gave him a dollar and the man left.

"What's that?"

"A telegram for the bank," Clint said. "I need to withdraw some money."

"The bank is right next to the apothecary, where I'm going," she said.

"Well then," he said, putting his napkin on the table, "let's go."

ELEVEN

Clint walked Andrea to the apothecary, then went to the bank next door. She was waiting outside for him when he came out.

"Get what you wanted?"

"I did," he said. "How about you?"

"My dad needed some things for a sick cow," she said.

"Does he always work on large animals?" he asked. "Cows, horses . . ."

"Oh, he treats smaller animals, too. Dogs, cats, he's even worked on wolves."

"What about you?" he asked as they started walking away from the bank.

"What do you mean?"

"Are you a vet?" he asked. "I mean, will you be a vet?"

"I don't have the training," she said.

"I'll bet you do from working with him," he said. "What you probably don't have are the credentials, the right to call yourself a vet."

"You're right," she said. "I'm his assistant, and I can do some of the things he does because I've watched and learned. I'm still watching and learning."

"Well, you're smart," Clint said. "You'll get what you want."

"Where are you off to now?" she asked. "Checking on your horse?"

"No, I did that already," he said. "I need to go and get some information."

"Is that what the money is for?"

"Some of it."

"Well," she said, "I hope you get what you want."

"So do I," he said. "I'll probably come over to your office tomorrow, though."

"This time I won't avoid you," she said.

"Promise?"

"I swear."

He smiled and she turned and walked away, toward her dad's office. Clint headed back to the saloon to buy his information.

When he entered the saloon, the bartender was there alone, wiping the bar with a rag. He looked up when he heard Clint come in.

"Back already?"

Clint walked to the bar and set some money on it. The bartender looked down at it.

"Count it," Clint said. "That's how much the information is worth to me."

"I don't have to count it," the bartender said. He swept the money off the bar, tucked it away underneath somewhere. "There was a fella in here last night who was quiet, until he had a few drinks. Then he began to talk."

"And who heard him talking?"

"Just me," the man said. "As you can see, we don't do a booming business here."

"So what did he have to say?"

"He was upset that some friend of his had got killed," the bartender said.

"Did he say when? Where?"

"When was real recent," the man said. "Where was some-where outside of town."

"Did he say by who?"

The bartender shook his head.

"Didn't say, and didn't really say what the circumstances were," the bartender said. "But I got the impression that his friend had been shot."

This was all close enough.

"Did he say his name?"

The man thought a moment, then said, "I don't think so."

"Would more money jog your memory?"

"No, no," the man said, smiling, "I ain't tryin' to jack up the price on ya. I just don't think he said his name."

"Was he staying in town?"

"He said he was staying at the rooming house."

"There's a rooming house in town?"

"Yep," the bartender said. "North end of town, Mrs. Nun-ally runs it."

"I knew about the two hotels . . ."

"Well, nobody mentions the rooming house because of them, but he musta found out about it somehow."

"Not from you?"

"No, but any bartender in town coulda told him about it," the bartender explained.

"I see," Clint said. "Anything else you can tell me about him?"

"Naw," the bartender said. "That's about all I got, mister. Honest."

"Okay," Clint said, "thanks."

He started to leave, then turned back. Sometimes it was the questions you didn't ask that got you killed.

"You got any idea who else is staying at the rooming house?" he asked. "Or how many guests she's got?"

The man thought a moment, then shook his head and said, "Naw, I dunno. I do know she's got about eight rooms, though."

"Eight, huh?" Clint said. "Okay, thanks, friend."
"No problem."

Clint left the saloon, wondering why Sheriff Ingram had not told him about the boardinghouse. Did he keep it to himself deliberately, or had it just slipped his mind? Or not occurred to him to mention?

He walked to the north end of town and located the two-story boardinghouse owned and operated by Mrs. Nunally. It stood alone, with no other houses around it. It certainly would have been his choice as a place to stay in town if he wanted to go unnoticed. Then again, he wouldn't have gone to a saloon and run off at the mouth after a few drinks.

He considered his options. He could go to the front door, knock, and ask if anyone had taken a room over the past two days. Or he could wait and watch as boarders came and went. Maybe he'd recognize someone. And maybe not. The only one of the three men who bushwhacked him he'd seen was the one he'd killed. The other men he'd have to recognize from somewhere else, like maybe Wells.

He decided to knock on the door.

TWELVE

"I don't have any rooms," the severe-looking woman who answered the door said.

"I'm not looking for a room."

"Then why are you bothering me?" she asked. "I have work to do."

"I just have a few questions."

She folded her chubby arm beneath her formidable bosom.

"Why should I answer questions?"

"Because you may have a killer in your house."

She dropped her hands.

"What do you mean?"

"Answer my questions and maybe I can tell you."

She hesitated, then said, "All right, ask. But you can't come in."

"I don't want to come in," Clint said. "Have you had a new boarder in the past two days?"

"Yes."

"What's his name?"

"Sands, Derrick Sands."

"Do you know where he's from?"

"No."

"Do you know where he is now?"

"I do not."

"He's not in his room?"

"He doesn't have a room here."

"I thought you said he was a boarder."

"He was. He is not anymore."

"When did he leave?"

"This morning."

"Did he say where he was going?"

"He didn't say, and I don't care," she said. "He was an unpleasant man. Now that you intimate he was a killer, I can see why."

"Where was he keeping his horse?"

"I don't know, the livery stable, I suppose."

Clint frowned. He had never gotten round to checking the livery stables. Maybe if he had, he would have found Derrick Sands.

Damn it.

"Okay, Mrs. Nunally," he said. "Thank you."

"Hmph," she said, and started to close the door.

"Oh, wait."

"Yes?"

"You said you had no rooms available," he said, "but that Sands left this morning."

"Well, I've still got to clean the room," she said. "I can't rent it the way it is."

"You mind if I take a look before you clean it?"

"Mister," she said, "I don't have all day to wait—"

"I'll give you five dollars."

She opened the door wide and said, "In advance."

She told him he could have five minutes for his five dollars. It was a high price, but five minutes were all he'd need.

He entered the room and saw what she meant. If the man had been in the room for two days—or even one—he was a slob. The sheets were soiled and all over the place. The drawers in the chest were hanging open, but they were empty.

He walked around, picked the sheets up off the floor, and a slip of paper fluttered out. He picked it up. It was a telegraph slip, the kind you filled out when you wanted to send a telegram. It said: Orwell, Texas. Nothing else.

Maybe it was enough.

Clint headed for the telegraph office, then remembered the clerk said he'd left some telegrams at the front desk of his hotel. He stopped there first and picked them up. One from Roper, one from Rick Hartman, both saying the same thing. They didn't know anything about a price being put out on Clint's head. That meant if it had been done, it had been done privately.

He pocketed the telegrams, then continued on to the telegraph office.

"You got more you wanna send?" the clerk asked as he entered.

"No," Clint said, handing him the slip he'd found in the room at the boardinghouse. "I want to know if this telegram was sent yesterday or today."

The clerk took it and read it.

"Oh yeah, I sent this."

"When?"

"Yesterday afternoon."

"Was there a reply?"

"No."

"Where did you send it to?"

The clerk thought a moment then said, "Kirby."

"Kirby, Texas?"

"That's right."

"Not Orwell?"

"No."

"And who did he sent it to?"

"I don't remember."

"Don't you have it written down somewhere?"

"Well," the clerk said, scratching his head, "I got it around here someplace."

"Can you look for it?" Clint asked.

"It might take a while."

"That's okay," Clint said.

From the telegraph office, Clint headed back to Doc Martin's office, after all. He needed to find out if he could ride Eclipse without doing any damage to the animal. If he was okay to ride, then Clint would be leaving for Orwell first thing in the morning. Hopefully, before then he'd have the name of the man Derrick Sands had sent a telegram to, and then he'd likely have the names of both of the men who had tried to kill him.

But first he had to make sure he had a horse, even if he had to rent one.

THIRTEEN

"Back so soon?" Doc Martin asked as he let Clint in.

"Something's come up," Clint explained.

"Oh? What's that?"

"I have to ride tomorrow," Clint said. "Can Eclipse travel?"

"How far?"

"I don't know," Clint said. "How far is Orwell?"

"Too far," Martin said. "That wound could open up and fester."

"I thought it wasn't bad."

"It's not," Martin said, "and I'd like to keep it that way."

"All right," Clint said. "I'll have to rent a horse."

"So you'll be back?"

"Of course," Clint said. "I'm not going to leave my horse here for good."

"No, of course not."

At that moment Andrea came walking in, carrying a basin and some bottles.

"Oh, I didn't expect to see you here."

"Just came by to ask a question," Clint said, "and I got my answer."

"What question?"

"I'm sorry," Clint said, "your father can tell you. I've got a lot to do."

"How long will you be gone?" Martin asked.

"I don't know," Clint said. "A day or two maybe."

"Well," Martin said, "we'll take good care of your horse while you're gone."

"Thank you," Clint said. He looked at Andrea and said again, "I'm sorry, I have to go."

He turned and went out the door. Andrea looked at her father, but he only shrugged.

"Sands?" Sheriff Ingram asked.

"Yes, Derrick Sands. Ever heard of him?"

"No, can't say I have."

"He had a room at Mrs. Nunally's boardinghouse," she said. "I think he was one of the men who tried to bushwhack me."

"What was he doing here in town?"

"I don't know."

"And you think he's meeting the other one in Orwell?" the lawman asked.

"According to his telegram," Clint said, "he's meeting somebody there."

"But he sent the telegram to Kirby."

"Yes. Where is Kirby?"

"Actually," Ingram said, "it's between here and Orwell."

"Then I'll be able to check Kirby on the way?" Clint asked.

"Sure, I suppose, if you want to. I mean, it's not on a straight line."

They were sitting in Ingram's office. Clint had turned down the offer of coffee.

"Where are your deputies?" Clint asked. "I've never seen them."

"One is making his rounds," Ingram said. "The other is out with my tracker, trying to find your men's trail."

"Maybe," Clint said, "when they do, it'll lead them to Orwell."

"Or here."

"Or Kirby," Clint said.

"When will you be leavin'?" Ingram asked.

"First thing in the morning," Clint said. "I'll be renting a horse. Mine's not ready for the trip."

"I can loan you a horse, save you some money."

"Your horse?"

"I have more than one," Ingram said. "Don't worry, it'll be a good one."

"Okay," Clint said, "I accept."

"I'll have it ready for you in the morning, out front," Ingram promised.

"Thanks."

Clint stood up.

"Where to now?"

"I've still got some things to do before I leave," Clint said.

"I'll buy you a drink tonight," Ingram said. "How about the Jack of Hearts?"

"Fine," Clint said. "I'll see you there later."

"Fine."

Clint left the office.

FOURTEEN

Clint went to his hotel to check with the clerk and see if the telegraph clerk had found the name.

"Sorry, sir," the man said, "no messages."

"Okay, thanks. Let me know as soon as one comes, though."

"Yes, sir."

"I'm going to be riding out of town tomorrow, but I want to keep my room. I'll be back in a few days."

"Whatever you say, sir."

Clint had intended to go to his room and pack his saddlebags, but for some reason today he had been hungry since the start of the day. Even after breakfast, and later pie. He decided to go into the dining room and have an early steak.

There were only a few tables taken, so he was served immediately. While he was eating, he thought about Maria and the night they'd had together. Maybe that's what had his appetite in an uproar. The girl had worked him hard.

He was finishing up when he saw the telegraph clerk come to the doorway and look around, When the clerk spotted Clint, he hotfooted it across the floor.

"I found that name, Mr. Adams!" he said excitedly.

"Good," Clint said. "What is it?"

The clerk looked at the piece of paper in his hand.

"Uh, it's Dunn, Adam Dunn." He looked at Clint. "I shoulda remembered that, since it's like your name."

"I get it," Clint said. "Can I have that?"

"Sure."

Clint took the piece of paper and handed the clerk a couple of dollars.

"Thanks!" the clerk said, and hurried back out.

Clint looked at the name on the slip of paper. He didn't recognize it, but now he had two names: Adam Dunn and Derrick Sands. And hopefully he'd find one or both of them in Orwell, Texas.

After he finished eating, he went back to the sheriff's office, but Ingram wasn't there. Behind the desk sat a young man with a deputy's badge.

"He ain't here, Mr. Adams," the deputy said. He swallowed hard, obviously intimidated by being in the presence of the Gunsmith.

"Do you know where I can find him?"

"No, sir," the deputy said. "He's just . . . out and about, I guess."

"Okay, well . . . just tell him I was looking for him, will you?"

"Sure, Mr. Adams," the deputy said. "Can I tell him what it was about?"

"Just tell him I have a name for him."

"Okay, I will."

"Thanks."

Clint left the office. Since he was depending on Ingram to get him a horse for the next morning, all he had left to do was go back to his room, pack his saddlebags, and make sure his weapons were in proper working order.

* * *

When he got to his room, it was getting on toward dusk. From beneath the door he saw light. He put his hand on his gun and opened the door.

Maria lay on the bed, stark naked with her eyes closed. Rather than pretending to be asleep, she writhed slowly while moving her hands over her body. She started at her breasts, rubbing them and playing with her nipples until they were erect. As she continued to tease herself, she purred softly as if she were alone in the room. Clint watched while he undressed, enjoying every second of the show she was giving him.

Her hands drifted down over her stomach as her legs opened wide. One hand eased down her thigh while the other went straight to the thatch of hair covering her slick little pussy. Arching her back when she touched herself, Maria ran her fingertips up and down to trace her pink lips. Clint couldn't wait another second before crawling onto the bed to start licking her. That seemed to genuinely surprise her, but Maria quickly began grinding against his face.

Clint's tongue brought her to a quick climax that sent shivers through her body. When she opened her eyes, she watched him settle on top of her and guide his erect penis toward her dripping wet slit. Maria reached down with both hands to open herself for him, and when he entered her, she placed her fingers on his shaft to feel him sliding in and out. Once he picked up speed, she moved her hands up onto his chest and wrapped her legs around him.

For several minutes, he savored the warmth of her skin and the touch of her nails against his body. She then wrapped her arms around him and held him close enough for Clint to feel the heat and firm, smooth texture of her breasts. Every time he pumped into her, she let out a short, groaning breath. Maria's hands roamed over Clint's back until she stretched her arms over her head to grab on to the iron bars of the bed's frame.

Clint rose up so he was kneeling between her legs. Still inside her, he held her legs and spread them open wide so he could start thrusting with building intensity. Maria's eyes remained closed but a smile crossed her lips. Leaning forward a bit, he placed his hands upon her breasts and massaged them as he pumped in and out of her. Maria's skin was hot and she moaned with pleasure as he rubbed his palms against her nipples.

Looking down, Clint drank in the sight of her. The sound of her breathy moans made his erection even harder. She squirmed so much and responded so intensely to everything he did that Clint got the sudden urge to drive her wild. Keeping one hand on her breast, he teased her nipple while reaching between her legs to rub her clit as he continued to drive into her. That caused her eyes to snap open and her voice to catch in her throat. It wasn't long at all before her entire body was rocked by a powerful climax. When she was through, Maria crawled out from under him and pushed Clint onto his back.

Taken by surprise by her sudden move, he was surprised again when she wrapped her lips around his cock and started bobbing her head up and down. She sucked him hungrily, eager to drive him just as wild as he'd driven her. As she ran her lips up and down his rigid pole, she raked her nails along his chest and stomach. Soon her entire body was in motion as if she meant to crawl on top of him without letting her mouth stop what it was doing.

Her mouth slid over every inch of his cock. When she brought her head up, Maria swirled her tongue around his tip until he took her head in his hands and kept her in that spot. Slowly, she began to suck him again. This time, she took every inch of him inside her mouth until her lips closed at the base of his shaft. Maria didn't move very much after that. She didn't have to. Her tongue was busy sending shivers down his spine until Clint thought he would burst.

She eased her head up and then bobbed up and down even faster than before. Clint could only take that for so long before his climax approached. He leaned back, let out a long breath, and let it happen. She drank him down, licked her lips, and asked for seconds a little while later.

FIFTEEN

"You did not come back to me for more, so I came to you,"
she said later, lying in the crook of his arm.

"I've been busy," he said. "Besides, it's only been a few
hours."

She slapped his arm and said sternly, "It has been all day,
bruto!"

"And don't you have to go to work?"

"I do," she said, "very soon. That is why I came to see you."

"Maria," Clint said, "I'm sorry, it's just . . . I have to leave
town tomorrow."

She sat up and looked down at him. He, in turn, looked
at her lovely breasts, the nipples still hard.

"So soon?"

"Not for good," he said. "I have to go to Orwell, but I'll
be back."

"Hmph," she said, lying back on the crook of his arm,
"so you say."

"It's true," he said. "My horse is still at the vet's."

"Ah," she said, "and you would not leave your horse, eh?"

"That's right."

"But you would leave me?"

"Maria—"

She laughed and slid her hand down over his belly.

"Do not worry, *hombre*," she said, "Maria is joking. I know we are only passing, eh? Lovers for the moment?"

Her words did make him relax, but her hand didn't. It continued to move lower until she was holding his cock in her hand—and he was filling it.

"This will have to be quick," she told him, slipping down between his legs. "I must go to work, but . . ." She licked her lips and swooped in on him . . .

It was quick and she was gone, leaving him pleasantly exhausted.

After a short time, he pulled on his pants and went about packing his saddlebags, and then cleaning his guns. He worked on all three, his modified Colt, his Winchester, and the little Colt New Line. He made sure they were all working. He was after two men, but by the time he caught up to them, they were liable to have joined up with some others. Bushwhackers had a pack mentality. They were cowards, and they felt safer in a group.

When he finished, he realized he was hungry again. It was past supper time, but he might find a café still open. He dressed, putting on the same shirt, and left his room.

Down the street he found a small restaurant that was still open. It wasn't late for saloons, but for restaurants it was different. Most of them had closed, the cooks and waiters and waitresses having gone home to their families.

Bartenders, saloon girls, gamblers, their lives really began when the sun went down.

"Closing?" he asked the waiter.

"Not while you're here, sir," the man said. "We don't turn away paying customers."

Clint sat and ordered a steak dinner. The waiter went into the kitchen, there was some shouting, and then a man in an apron stormed out. The waiter came out after him.

"Who was that?" Clint asked.

The cook," the waiter said, "but don't worry, I can make a steak."

"I don't want to cause trouble—"

"That was my partner," the man said. "He has a big ego, and he's always storming out. He'll be back tomorrow. Sit back and relax. I'll make you a steak."

"Okay, thanks."

It took a while, but the man finally came out holding a plate with a steak and vegetables on it.

"There ya go."

Clint stared at it.

"I hope you like your meat well done."

"I've had well-done steaks before," he said.

Glumly, the man said, "And that's not well done, right? It's burnt." He sat down opposite Clint. "I'm sorry. I really can't cook."

"I can," Clint said. He stood and picked up the plate. "Come on."

SIXTEEN

Clint cooked two steak dinners, and while they weren't perfect, they were better than the burnt steak the man had served him.

The waiter's name was Tom Hamilton, and with his partner, George Manning—who was also the cook—he owned the café.

They sat together and ate their food.

"Wow," Hamilton said, "this is better than anything I coulda made. Where'd you learn to cook?"

"Comes from living alone," Clint said. "Plus I don't have a partner who can cook."

"George's steaks are always perfect," Hamilton said, then quickly added, "No offense. This is fine."

"No offense taken," Clint assured him.

"I don't recognize you," Hamilton said. "New in town?"

"Been here a day or so," Clint said, "but I've got to ride out in the morning."

"Too bad," Hamilton said. "You should meet George—I mean, when he's in a better mood."

"What was he so upset about?" Clint asked.

"He was ready to douse the stove and close up when you came in," Hamilton said.

"Sorry I caused trouble."

"That's okay," Hamilton said.

When they were done, Clint asked, "Want me to help clean up?"

"Naw," Hamilton said, picking up the plates, "that's my specialty."

"Well, then . . . thanks. Maybe I'll stop in again when I get back."

"Comin' back?"

"Yeah, I'll be back in a day or two."

"See ya then."

The two men shook hands and Clint left the café. He went back to his hotel, read for a short while, then turned in for the night so he could get an early start in the morning.

Maria did not return during the night, which was fine with him. He'd had a good night's sleep—probably the best he'd had in some time.

He woke up the next morning, dressed, and went down to the lobby. He found the dining room open early, so he stopped in there for breakfast before walking to the sheriff's office.

In front of the office was one horse, a big steeldust, already saddled. The animal looked like a sturdy five- or six-year-old. Clint wasn't certain that this was the horse he'd be riding, but if it was, he was satisfied. Also with the saddle, which was a fine-looking McClellan.

He opened the office door and stepped in.

"See your horse?" Sheriff Ingram asked.

"That steeldust?"

"That's him."

"Good-looking animal."

"Should do the job for you." Ingram was behind his desk. "Sorry you didn't find me last night. Deputy said you were here. You find a name?"

"Yeah, Adam Dunn. Mean anything to you?"

Ingram thought a moment, then said, "Naw, nothing. I'll check and see if there's any paper on him."

"I'll check in with the sheriff in Orwell when I get there," Clint said.

"I can send him a telegram and tell him you're comin'," Ingram said.

"I'd appreciate that."

"Oh," Clint said, "and thanks for the saddle. I was going to put my own on the horse."

"Still can if you want," Ingram said. "I just thought I'd have him ready for you to go."

"I'll take him as is," Clint said. "Got a name?"

"He answers to Dusty." Ingram stood up, grabbed his hat. "I'll walk out with you."

The two men went outside, stood in front of the office looking at the horse.

"What is he? Five?"

"Six."

Clint walked to the horse, patted his neck, then tossed his saddlebags over him. He checked the cinch on the saddle, found it nice and tight.

"Well, thanks for everything, Sheriff," Clint said. "I hope I'll be able to settle my problem in Orwell, and then I'll bring back your horse."

Ingram put his hand out and the two men shook.

"Good luck," he said. "I know the sheriff in Orwell. He's a good man. His name's Paul Roberts. I'll send that telegram right away."

"Thanks." Clint mounted the horse, liked the way it felt underneath him.

"Push him as hard as you like," Ingram said. "He can take it."

"I'll bet he can," Clint said, patting the horse's neck. "Okay, Dusty, let's get a move on."

He pulled on the reins, turning the horse, then waved at the sheriff and rode up the street, heading out of town.

* * *

Sheriff Ingram waited until Clint Adams was out of sight, then stepped down off the boardwalk and walked to the telegraph office to send that telegram to Orwell, Texas. Sheriff Paul Roberts would be very interested to hear that the Gunsmith was coming to his town. Very interested, indeed.

SEVENTEEN

Clint stopped off in Kirby first, a small town that—for some reason—had a telegraph office.

Clint rode in, stopped in front of the office right away. He had no intention of staying any longer than he had to. He tied the horse off and went inside.

"Help ya?" the older clerk asked. He had gray hair and was missing one of his front teeth.

"Do you remember receiving this telegram?" Clint asked. He showed him the slip of paper with "Orwell, Texas" written on it.

"You law?"

"I'm not."

"Then who's askin'?"

"My name's Clint Adams."

The clerk swallowed and asked, "T-The Gunsmith?"

"That's right."

"I got this telegram yesterday," he said quickly. "Gave it to the feller and he left town."

"Fellow named Dunn?"

"Dunn, yeah, that's right, Adam Dunn—like your last name."

Clint nodded. "He left town right away?"

"Walked outta here, got on his horse, and rode out."

"Okay," Clint said, folding the slip of paper and putting it in his pocket, "thanks."

"Sure thing."

Clint walked out and mounted Sheriff Ingram's steeldust. So far, the horse had done everything Clint had asked. He turned the horse, preparing to ride out, when the clerk came out the door.

"Mr. Adams?"

"Yeah?"

"There's somethin' else ya might wanna know."

Clint turned the horse to face the man.

"What's that?"

"When Dunn left, he didn't leave alone."

That was interesting to Clint.

"How many?"

"He had three men with him."

"You know who they were?"

"Just gunnies for hire," the clerk said. "Not local."

The three men had probably met Dunn there. What about Sands, then? Had he left Hastings alone, or had he also picked up a few men?

Suddenly, Clint was thinking maybe that piece of paper he'd found in Sands's room with Orwell written on it had not been left behind by accident.

Clint dug a silver dollar out of his pocket and flipped it to the clerk, who caught it neatly in one hand.

"Thanks for the information."

"Sure thing."

Clint turned Dusty around and rode out of town.

It was getting on toward dusk when Clint got to Orwell. He reined Dusty in and looked at the town as the lights began to come on. If Dunn and Sands were waiting for him there with extra men, it would be better for him to ride in after dark, so he dismounted, sat on a rock to wait. The steeldust nuzzled him, so he rubbed the horse's nose and spoke to him soothingly.

"Don't worry, fella," he said, "we'll be riding in soon."

He'd go in and see the sheriff first. He knew Ingram was going to send the man a telegram about him, but he didn't know what else he'd tell him, whether or not he'd mention Sands and Dunn—and only Clint knew about the extra men.

He took out a piece of beef jerky and chomped on it while he waited. Finally, it was fully dark, and he mounted up again and rode into the town of Orwell.

Four men sat together in a saloon in Orwell, passing around a bottle of whiskey.

"Take it easy on that stuff," one of them said.

"Why?" another asked. "The Gunsmith ain't gonna be fool enough to ride at night, is he? If he ain't here by now, he'll be here sometime tomorrow."

"If he's comin' here at all," one of the other men said.

"Hey," the first man said, "we're only gettin' paid if he shows up, so he better." He grabbed the bottle of whiskey. "And you guys better be sober when he gets here!"

"Hey, give that here!"

"You should be out there watchin' the street," the first man said.

"I wanna drink!"

"You had enough, Pierce," said the first man, whose name was Mike Torrey. "Now get out there and watch the street. Let us know if anybody—and I mean anybody—rides in."

Pierce stood up, shifted his holster, and trudged toward the batwing doors, muttering, "This is stupid. Ain't nobody gonna ride in at night."

He stepped outside, just missing the Gunsmith, who had ridden by only seconds before.

Clint reined in his horse in front of the sheriff's office. Tied Dusty's reins off to a hitching post, and stepped to the door.

He knocked, and entered when a man's gruff voice yelled, "Come in, already!"

Clint stepped inside. A man holding a broom stopped sweeping and looked at him. He was wearing a badge.

"Sheriff Roberts?" he asked.

"That's right. You Adams?"

"I am."

"Didn't think you'd be ridin' in at night." Sheriff Roberts put the broom aside. "Well, you better have a seat and tell me what this is all about."

EIGHTEEN

"How much did Sheriff Ingram tell you in his telegram?" Clint asked.

"Not much, just that you'd be comin' here." Sheriff Roberts got himself comfortable behind his desk. He was a barrel-chested fellow in his forties. His gun belt and hat were hanging on pegs on the wall.

"Well, a couple of days ago three men tried to bushwhack me . . ." Clint told Roberts the whole story, finishing up with the information he'd gotten when he stopped in Kirby.

"So they're here? With a gang?"

"You haven't seen a bunch of men ride in?" Clint asked.

"If they rode in, they didn't come in all at once," Roberts said. "If they were smart, they came in one or two at a time."

"Do you know of any strangers who came to town today?"

"A few," Roberts said, "but I had no reason to brace them when they did. Maybe now, though, it's a different story."

"I rode in after dark on purpose," Clint said, "just in case they were watching, and waiting."

"Chances are if they all met up, they did it in one of the saloons," Roberts said. "I guess we oughtta go and check that out."

"And then do what?" Clint asked. "If we find them, I mean."

"Run 'em out of town," Roberts said.

"First I'd like to find out if my men are among them," Clint said. "Sands or Dunn."

Roberts stood up, grabbed his gun belt and hat, and put them on.

"We might as well take a walk. Before we decide what to do, let's see if they're here."

Pierce was scowling as he looked up and down the street. Chewing on a toothpick. When he looked to his left, he saw two men walking down the street. It was dark, and the streetlamps weren't doing such a good job of lighting the street, but he thought he saw a badge on one man's chest.

He turned and hurried through the batwings.

"Did you see that?" Roberts asked.

"I did," Clint said. "Looks like they may have had a man on watch."

"How do you want to play this?" the lawman asked.

"I think I should go in the front," Clint said. "You take the back."

"My town," Roberts said. "I should go in the front."

"They won't try anything," Clint said. "They're not after you. It's me they want."

"Okay, then," Roberts said. "You go in the front, I'll take the back."

"Okay."

Roberts grabbed Clint's left arm.

"I know your rep, Adams," he said, "but Sheriff Ingram vouched for you, which is the only reason I'm lettin' you call the play. Got it?"

"I've got it, Sheriff."

"Good luck, then. Give me 'til a count of ten and I'll be in place."

"Right."

They split, the sheriff moving alongside the building to the back.

Clint approached the front of the saloon, slowly counting to ten. One . . . two . . .

"Law comin'!" Pierce said as he rushed into the saloon.

"Alone?" Mike Torrey asked.

"No," Pierce said, "got a man with him."

"Okay, don't panic," Torrey said. "He's probably just makin' his regular rounds."

"Where do you want us, Mike?" one of the men sitting with him asked.

"Split up," Torrey said. "Tate, you and Holcomb at opposite ends of the bar."

"And me?" Pierce asked.

"In the back," Torrey said, "and don't panic. Nobody shoots unless I do. Got it?"

"We got it," Tate said.

"Pierce?"

"I got it!"

"Then move."

Torrey watched the three men get into position. The only one he worried about was Pierce. He, Holcomb, and Tate had ridden into Orwell with Dunn. It was the other fella, Sands, who had brought Pierce in. Torrey didn't trust Pierce at all.

He remained seated at the table, poured himself a glass of whiskey, and watched the door.

Seven . . . eight . . .

The sheriff reached the back of the saloon and opened the rear door, which he knew from experience was never locked. He entered, closed it quietly, and crept across the expanse of the back storeroom until he came to another door. From there he could see the inside of the small saloon.

He settled in to do what the men in the saloon were doing . . . wait.

Nine . . . ten.

Clint stepped up onto the boardwalk and approached the front door of the saloon. It was quiet inside. No music. No sounds of men cursing and gambling.

Just the silence of a bunch of men . . .

. . . waiting.

NINETEEN

Clint stepped inside.

The saloon was less than half filled—a few men at the bar, some more seated at tables. However, there were no men clustered at the bar together, or at a table. If there were three or four men there who were out for him, they weren't showing themselves.

But he'd dealt with these men all his life. He looked around the room and picked out the four likeliest ones. They were the four who were paying the most attention to him, but trying not to show it. Also, the bartender was very nervous.

This had to be the right place.

There was a man sitting at a table alone with a bottle of whiskey and four glasses.

Clint walked to the table.

"Bad idea to leave all the glasses on the table, friend," he said. "It's kind of a dead giveaway."

"Don't know what you're talkin' about, friend."

"Yeah, I think you do," Clint said. The question is, where are the other two? Or are you Dunn? Sands?"

"My name's Torrey," the man said. "Mike Torrey, and I don't know you."

"Well," Clint said, "now's the time to get acquainted."

The man swallowed, risked a look at the bar.

"I count three more," Clint said. "If any of them go for their guns, I'll get you first."

"Now wait a minute—"

"Where are Sands? Dunn? Are they here?"

"No."

"So they just hired you to wait for me?"

"It's just business, Adams, you know? Nothing personal."

"Sorry," Clint said, "but when somebody tries to kill me, I take it very personal."

"Look," Torrey said, "it's all set up. If either one of us makes the wrong move, there's gonna be a lot of lead flyin'."

"Then maybe we shouldn't make the wrong move," Clint said. "Just tell me where they are."

"Sands and Dunn?"

Clint nodded.

"If I tell you, you ain't gonna like it."

"Try me."

"They're in Hastings."

Clint hesitated, then said, "You're right, I don't like it."

Shrugging, Torrey took a drink from his glass, which Clint noticed he was holding with his left hand.

"So we don't have to do this," Clint said.

"That's up to you," Torrey said. "Just turn around and walk out if you want."

"You think your friends will go along with that?" Clint asked.

"They have orders not to fire unless I do."

"I'm going to back out," Clint said. "Let's try not to get anybody killed."

Torrey shrugged again. He already had the money Dunn had paid him, and Dunn was in Hastings, as he had told the Gunsmith. He really didn't care.

"Go ahead . . ."

* * *

Their conversation could be heard by everyone in the place, and while Tate and Holcomb were willing to go along with whatever Torrey said, Tom Pierce was apparently not.

Pierce, watching Clint back toward the batwings, thought that his chance would soon be going out the door, so although he did it nervously, he reached for his gun . . .

From his position in the back of the room, Sheriff Roberts saw Pierce going for his gun. He turned the barrel of his rifle that way and fired.

And all hell broke loose . . .

After the sheriff's shot, all three of the other men went for their guns. Clint was almost to the doors when he saw them draw.

He drew his own gun and fired . . .

Torrey, angry that someone other than him had called the play, stood up, drew his gun, and flipped the table over for cover.

The other two, Tate and Holcomb, had no such cover. As they drew, Clint turned the barrel of his gun on them and shot each of them.

Clint knew Torrey hadn't called the play. He'd had his eyes on the man the whole time. Torrey was behind the fallen table, and Clint decided to wait and see what the man was going to do.

The sheriff, however, had no such intentions. He stepped out of the doorway into the saloon, leveled his rifle at Torrey, and fired. The bullet took the man in the back. He straightened up, staggered, and fell over the fallen table.

The other men in the place—including the frightened bartender—had all hit the floor. Now that the shooting had stopped, they began to raise their heads.

"Everybody out!" Sheriff Roberts shouted.

The bystanders rose and ran out of the saloon.

The bartender stood where he was.

"Cliff," Roberts said, "two whiskeys."

"Comin' up, Sheriff."

Clint checked all the bodies to make sure they were dead, then joined the sheriff at the bar.

"That one in the back drew," the lawman said. "I had no choice."

Clint picked up his whiskey and said, "I almost got out with no bloodshed."

"Talked them out of it, did ya?" Roberts asked.

"That one seemed to be the leader, and we came to an understanding," Clint said.

"Are any of these men the ones you were lookin' for?" Roberts asked.

"Apparently not," Clint said. "That one told me that Sands and Dunn are in Hastings."

"Well, if you were in Hastings with them, why'd they get you out here?"

"That's what I'm going to find out when I get back," Clint said.

"Not gonna ride at night, are ya?"

"No," Clint said, "I'll put up my horse, get a room, and head out first thing."

The two men drank down their whiskeys.

"Another one," Roberts said to the bartender.

"Not for me," Clint said. "I want to get an early start in the morning."

"I'll have these bodies taken care of," Roberts said.

"Will you need a statement from me?" Clint asked.

"Naw, I was here," Roberts said. "I'll take care of everything."

"I appreciate it, Sheriff," Clint said.

He turned and looked down at the dead men. It didn't sit right with him that the sheriff had shot Torrey in the back, but he couldn't concern himself with that at the moment. He was smarting from being bamboozled by Dunn and Sands into riding all the way to Orwell to kill four men.

Tomorrow he'd show them just how much he resented it.

TWENTY

Clint rode out the next morning without seeing Sheriff Roberts again. He was in a hurry to get back to Hastings, and he pushed the steeldust as hard as he could.

He bypassed Kirby and got back to Hastings late in the afternoon. Stopping at the sheriff's office, he was told by the deputy that Ingram was out, so he left the horse in front of the office. He would have unsaddled the horse, brushed, and fed it, but he didn't know where the sheriff kept his animals, and the deputy didn't feel comfortable telling him.

From the sheriff's office, Clint went back to his hotel.

"Back so soon, sir?" the clerk asked.

"That's right," Clint said. "Any messages?"

"No, sir."

He went up to his room to drop off his rifle and saddlebags, then came back down and headed for the vet's office. On the way he passed the undertaker's and decided to stop in.

"Yes, sir," the undertaker said, "the sheriff told me who you are. What can I do for you?"

"The body of the man I killed, is it still here?"

"Why, yes," the man said. "Why would it not be?"

"I've learned that the man's friends are still in town," Clint said. "I thought they may have claimed it."

"No one has claimed it, sir, and I need to do something with it soon."

"You got a potter's field?"

"We do."

"Then plant it," Clint said.

"Yes, sir," the undertaker said, "as you say."

Clint left the undertaker's office and continued on to the vet's office. When he got there, the front door was open, and he heard voices inside. When he entered, he was surprised to see the sheriff there, talking to Doc Martin and Andrea.

"What's going on?" he asked.

"You're back," Ingram said. "That's good."

"Oh, Clint . . . I'm so sorry," Andrea said.

"Sorry? About what?"

"It's your horse . . ." Martin said.

"What happened?' he demanded.

"They took him!" Andrea said. "They took Eclipse."

"Who took him?"

"Two men," she said.

Clint looked at Ingram.

"Dunn and Sands," Clint said.

"The two men you went to Orwell to find?"

"They weren't there," Clint said. "They suckered me into going there, where four men were waiting for me."

"What happened?"

"I killed them, with the help of the sheriff. Then I rushed back here, because before he died, one of them told me they were here. I guess now I know why." He looked at Andrea and her father. "How did they get him to go with them? Normally, Eclipse would never—"

"They threatened to kill my father if I didn't walk him outside and tie him to the back of a wagon," she said. "I—I couldn't refuse. I'm sorry."

"We're both sorry," Martin said, "but it's my fault. That horse was my responsibility."

"It's all right," Clint said. "Don't worry about it. I'll get him back."

"Are you sure?" Andrea asked.

"I'll get him back, and I'll find out why they took him," Clint said. He looked at Ingram. "If they harm that horse, they're dead."

"I understand," the lawman said. "Come on, let's go to my office and talk about our next move."

"*Our* next move?"

"Horse stealin' is a crime, isn't it?" Ingram said. "It's my job to get him back."

They left Martin and Andrea standing together, looked crestfallen.

"You really can't blame them for this," Ingram said as they walked out.

"I don't," Clint said. "I blame Dunn and Sands."

"You find out what they looked like?"

"Everything went south pretty quick," Clint said. "I never did get a description."

"Too bad."

"But we can get one of Sands from Mrs. Nunally."

"Fine," the sheriff said. "Let's go and do that right now." They changed direction and headed for the rooming house.

TWENTY-ONE

When Mrs. Nunally answered her door, she scowled at the two of them. Clint figured she was probably always an unpleasant woman.

"What do you want now?" she asked. Clint wasn't sure if she was asking him, or the lawman.

"The man I talked to you about last time I was here," Clint said. "Your tenant. What did he look like?"

"How should I know—"

"You rented him a room, ma'am," the sheriff said. "You should know what he looked like."

Still scowling she said, "Tall, thin, dirty, in his thirties. And he stank."

"Anything else?" Clint asked.

"Ain't that enough?"

"Did you ever see him with another man?" Clint asked.

"Yeah, one other. Same type, dirty, but younger, and nervous looking."

"Nothing else?" Ingram asked.

"Yeah," she said, "he was left-handed. That's all I got." She slammed the door.

"That help?" Ingram asked.

"A little," Clint said. "One of the men I killed in Orwell was left-handed."

They turned and walked away from the boardinghouse.

When they got to the sheriff's office, he said to the deputy, "Go make your rounds, Jody."

"It ain't my turn, Sheri—"

"Just do it!"

"Yes, sir." The deputy grabbed his hat and headed for the door.

"And see to my horse!"

"Yessir!"

Ingram picked up the coffeepot, found it empty.

"Damn it! I tol' them both that part of their job is keepin' this full."

He poured some water in the pot. Dumped in a couple of handfuls of coffee, and put it on the stove.

"What about your other deputy?" Clint asked. "The one who was out with the tracker? They find anything?"

"My tracker says your men were pretty good at hidin' their tracks. But he's pretty sure at least one of them went to Kirby."

"And the other?"

"He says he probably stayed here."

"The one who took a room at Mrs. Nunally's."

"But now you're sayin' they're both here," Ingram said.

"Well, somebody took my horse."

"Yeah, right."

"I'll need your tracker."

"What for?"

"To track them from the doc's office."

"The street is filled with wagon tracks."

"Is your man any good?"

"Plenty good," Ingram said, "but I don't know if anybody is that good."

"Well," Clint said, "why don't we find out."

"Okay," Ingram said, "I'll get ahold of him today."

"When?"

"When my deputy comes back."

"Not good enough," Clint said. "Tell me who he is and where I can find him."

"His name's Cain," Ingram said. "He's a half-breed. He's usually at the Wagon Wheel. That's a small saloon at the south end of town. Nobody ever goes there."

"Then why will I find him there?"

"Because he doesn't like people," Ingram said. "He won't like you."

"I'll tell him you sent me."

Ingram laughed.

"He doesn't like me either."

"Who does he like?"

"I've never been able to figure that out."

"Then why does he work for you?"

"I pay him."

"So I'll pay him."

"You best lead off with that fact."

Clint nodded, headed for the door just as the smell of coffee filled the room.

"Oh," he said, "how will I know him?"

"You'll know him," Ingram said. "You ain't seen anybody like him before."

TWENTY-TWO

Clint found the Wagon Wheel Saloon at the end of town. It was in a building that looked like it was a good stiff breeze away from falling down. As he approached the batwings, he saw that one was hanging sideways on one hinge, ready to fall. He entered carefully, not wanting to be the one who knocked it off.

Inside he saw two people, a bartender and a customer. Even if there had been twenty more, though, he would have known that this customer was the man he was looking for.

Tall—beyond tall, probably close to seven feet—rangy, wearing a long black duster and a black hat with a feather in it. He was bent over a glass of whiskey, with a bottle close at hand. There was also a Winchester on the bar, which Clint assumed belonged to the big man.

The bartender was a broad, beefy man with hairy arms and dark circles under his eyes. He watched as Clint approached the bar.

"You're in the wrong place," the bartender said.

"I'm looking for a beer."

"Like I said," the barman answered, "wrong place. There are other saloons."

Clint looked around and said, "I like this one."

"Why?"

"Because this is where I'm supposed to find Cain."

"Who says?"

"Sheriff Ingram."

"Why do you need him?"

"For work."

"You payin'?"

"I am."

"How much?"

"The goin' rate."

"For what?"

"For what he does," Clint said. "Tracking."

"Who are you?"

"My name's Clint Adams," Clint said. "I got bushwhacked outside of town. Ingram said he had Cain trying to track the men who tried to kill me. He figures one went to Kirby, and one stayed here."

"So what do you need?"

"They stole my horse," Clint said. "I want to get him back."

"Bad business," the big man said, "stealin' a man's horse."

The voice was deep, came rumbling out of his mouth as if from a deep cave.

"Yeah, it is," Clint replied, turning to face him.

When the man looked up, Clint saw that his eyes were green and startling, his lips thick and red. He had the red skin of an Indian, which made the eyes even more startling.

"Stole from where?"

"The vet's."

"Doc Martin?"

"Yes."

Cain stared at Clint, thinking, then said, "I will help you."

"For how much?"

"I thought you said the going rate."

"I did."

"Then that."

"Okay."

Cain turned to the bar and poured himself another drink.

"Uh, when?" Clint asked.

"I thought you said you wanted a beer."

"I do."

"I can't track at night," Cain said. He looked at the bartender. Give him a beer, Max."

"Yeah, okay."

"A cold one."

Max hesitated, then said, "Yeah, okay."

He put a beer on the bar for Clint.

"I appreciate the help," he said to Cain.

"You are paying me," Cain said. "That is appreciation enough."

"Yeah, I guess . . ."

Cain looked at him.

"I know who you are," he said, "and I know the sheriff sent you to me. Otherwise I would not have even spoken to you."

"I still appreciate it."

"Drink your beer," Cain said. "I will meet you tomorrow morning at the vet's office."

"Okay," Clint said, assuming he'd been dismissed. He drank the beer and left the saloon.

TWENTY-THREE

Clint spent a restless night. He was worried about Eclipse. He assumed Dunn and Sands had taken the horse so that he'd follow them, try to get him back. But if they had already harmed him . . .

At first light he got dressed, still not having slept very much. He went downstairs to the dining room to have breakfast. While he was eating, Sheriff Ingram came in.

"Join me?" Clint asked.

"Don't mind if I do," Ingram said.

Clint held up two fingers to the waiter, who brought over two plates of steak and eggs.

"I spoke to Cain," the sheriff said.

"Before or after I did?" Clint asked.

"After," Ingram said. "If you don't mind, I'll come along to Doc Martin's."

"I don't mind," Clint said. "I can use the help. I'm tracking two men, but there's no telling how many I'll find."

"That's what I figured."

After breakfast they walked over to Doc Martin's. Cain was already there, down on one knee in front of the big double doors on the side of the building. The doors were open, and the doc and his daughter, Andrea, were standing there, watching the big half-breed. They looked up as Clint and Ingram approached.

"Mornin', Doc, Andrea," Ingram said.

"Mornin', Sheriff," Martin said.

Andrea didn't speak, but she nodded at Clint.

Now the four of them watched as Cain read the ground.

"A lot of tracks here," he said, but nobody replied. It seemed he was talking to himself.

He got to his feet, but stayed bent over as he seemed to follow some tracks into the street. Clint looked both ways anxiously. He was afraid the big man might get run over by a wagon, but there was no traffic coming.

Finally, Cain looked up at Clint, as if he were the only person there.

"Can you do it?" Clint asked.

"I don't know anyone else who could," Cain said, "but I can. We'll need horses."

Clint looked at Ingram.

"Can I use Dusty again?"

"He's yours," the lawman said.

"I will get my horse and meet you back here," Cain said.

"Okay."

The big man walked away, his coat flapping behind him.

"He is a scary man," Andrea said.

"Good," Clint said, "I can use a scary man."

"He's a helluva tracker, though," Ingram said. "I'll get you that steeldust."

Ingram walked away and Doc Martin said, "Would you like to come in for a cup of coffee while you wait?"

"I'd like that, thanks."

Clint went inside with the vet and his daughter.

While Cain was saddling his horse in the livery, the sheriff came walkin' in behind him, leading his horse.

"I need you to do somethin' for me, Cain."

The half-breed turned to face the lawman.

"What is it?"

Ingram produced a deputy's badge.

"Wear this."

"Why?"

"When you find these men the Gunsmith is lookin' for," Ingram said, "I need you to keep him from killin' them."

"I can do that."

"I think it would be easier for you to do if you're official," the sheriff said.

Cain stared at the badge.

"I know you don't like badges," Ingram said. "Wear it as a favor to me."

Cain studied the tin in Ingram's hand for a few more moments, then took it. He didn't, however, pin it on.

"I'll take it, and carry it," he said, "but I won't put it on."

"As long as when the time comes, you show it," Ingram said.

Cain nodded and put the badge in his pocket.

"Do you really think this Indian can help you find Eclipse?" Andrea asked.

"He seems to know what he's doing," Clint said, "so I hope so."

"I hope so, too," Doc Martin said. "I'm feelin' really guilty about this."

"Don't," Clint said. "Apparently this was well planned. In fact, I'm not really sure these two men could have planned it themselves."

"You think someone is behind this?" Martin asked.

"Lately," Clint said, "I feel like people are comin' at me, even more than they used to."

"This is the life you've had to live with," Martin said, "isn't it?"

"In the past," Clint said, "they've come at me lookin' for a reputation. Lately, it seems more personal."

"That must be a hard way to have to live," Andrea said with a lot of sympathy in her voice.

"It is," Clint said. "I seemed to be able to handle it better when I was younger. Now I just keep thinking, who hates me that much? And why?"

"You want to sweeten that a bit?" Martin asked, indicating the cup of coffee in Clint's hand.

"Why not?"

Martin took out a bottle of whiskey and poured a dollop into his coffee, and Clint's.

"What do you plan to do when you catch up to them?" the vet asked.

"You might think I want to kill them right away," Clint said, "and I can't say I don't. When somebody tries to back-shoot me, that's my first reaction. But I need to find out who put them up to this."

"I can see that," Martin said. "In fact, I can understand either way that you go."

"But killing . . ." Andrea said, shaking her head.

"You can't understand that?" Clint asked.

"I can't understand killing another human being, no matter the reason," she said.

"Well then," Clint said, "I guess you just can't understand me at all."

"I don't understand your whole life," she said. "Your reputation just doesn't match the man I've met."

"There's not much I can do about that," Clint said. "The reputation is there, it's been there a long time. It's part of me."

He could tell by the look on Andrea's face that she was still not getting it. That was okay, though. She didn't have to.

Clint was the one who had to understand himself.

TWENTY-FOUR

Cain returned with his horse, a big Appaloosa. Moments later Ingram came walking up, leading Dusty, his steeldust.

Clint, Martin, and Andrea were waiting outside for them. Clint had the feeling that something had gone on between the two men while they were away. Of course, that could just be because they were friends—if they were, in fact, friends. Ingram certainly had respect for Cain's abilities, and Cain seemed to respect the lawman.

Ingram handed the reins to Clint, who mounted up. Sitting on his Appaloosa, Cain seemed to be even bigger.

"Do we need some supplies?" Clint asked.

"Don't know," Cain said. "Let's just see where these tracks lead us."

"Okay," Clint said. "Lead the way."

"Good luck," Doc Martin said.

"Let me know if you need anythin' from me," Ingram told them.

"We will," Clint said.

Cain started off, giving the horse his head as he stared down at the ground. Clint didn't know how he was picking out their particular set of wagon wheel tracks, but he followed.

* * *

Clint couldn't believe how Cain was able to follow the wagon tracks down the main street, which was filled with ruts and tracks from days of traffic.

When they reached the end of town, Cain drew his horse to a halt. Clint rode up alongside him and stopped.

"The tracks become more clear here."

"How the hell did you follow them this far?"

"It's your horse," Cain said. "He's trailin' along behind the wagon. I am following him."

"What is there about his track that makes him easy to follow?" Clint asked. "I've never noticed a particular marking in his hooves myself."

"It is the size," Cain said. And that was all.

"Should we keep going?" Clint asked.

"I think," Cain said, "we need some supplies."

They returned to town for a few supplies, just enough so that they could make camp if they had to. They didn't bother checking in with Sheriff Ingram. They made their purchases at the mercantile, and then rode right out of town again.

At the edge of town, Cain once again located the tracks left by the wagon and Eclipse, and they took up the chase again.

Derrick Sands entered the cabin as Adam Dunn was pouring some coffee.

"So?" Dunn asked.

"That animal is a devil," Sands said. "I don't know how we got it this far."

"Well, the girl helped," Dunn said. "She kept him calm."

"Yeah, well, it ain't calm now."

"Who's out there with him?"

"Sonora."

"Good," Dunn said, "he's our best handler."

Sands sat down at the table, poured himself a cup of coffee.

"Do you really think this is the way to go?" he asked.

"Why not?" Dunn asked. "Adams needs that horse. The trail will lead him right here. And we have enough men to take care of him."

"Yeah," Sands said, "we thought we left enough men in Orwell to take care of him."

"The problem there was, we weren't there," Dunn said. "I'm sure it all went wrong because of that idiot you recruited."

"Pierce?"

Dunn nodded.

"Yeah, you're probably right," Sands said, "but he was the best I could do."

"Well," Dunn said, "the men we have now are better. Don't worry, it's all gonna work out."

"I hope so," Sands said. "I really wanna get paid for this job."

"Don't worry, we will. We get him in this canyon and he won't have a chance."

Clint was surprised—and yet he wasn't—when the trail led to Kirby, the town where Sands had sent Dunn a telegram.

"Did they stop here?" Clint asked. They had stopped just on the outside of town.

"I will have to look around," Cain said. "I will see if they rode through town, or if they stopped somewhere."

"I'll stop in and see the local law," Clint said. "Do you know him?"

"No, I do not," Cain said. "I do not even know his name."

"Okay," Clint said, "I'll go and introduce myself to him, tell him what's going on."

"First you must decide if you trust him," Cain said.

"I know that," Clint said. "Believe me, I've learned not to trust a man just because he's wearing a badge."

At the mention of a badge, Cain put his hand on his pocket for some reason, but didn't say anything.

"Where should we meet?" Clint asked.

"Saloon." "Which one?"

"Whichever one has the least amount of people in it," Cain said.

"Gotcha," Clint said.

The two men split up there, Cain searching for more tracks, Clint looking for the sheriff's office.

TWENTY-FIVE

The front door of the sheriff's office was riddled with bullet holes. As Clint entered, he saw corresponding bullet holes in the wall across from the door. None of the holes were recent, however.

The man seated behind the desk had one bare foot up on the desktop, and was working on the nail of his big toe. He stopped what he was doing and looked up.

"What can I do for you?"

"You the sheriff?"

"I am."

"Lots of holes in that door."

"This used to be a wide-open town."

"And now?"

"Now it ain't."

"Because of you?"

"That's right." The sheriff looked at his foot, and smiled. "Oh, don't let this fool ya. I just got this hangnail that's been drivin' me crazy."

"Uh-huh."

"And who are you?"

"My name's Clint Adams."

"No shit?"

"No shit."

The sheriff dropped his foot off the desk to the floor.

"What's the Gunsmith doin' in my town?"

"Looking for two men."

"Who are they?"

"Derrick Sands and Adam Dunn."

The sheriff thought a moment.

"Don't know 'em."

"Maybe they're here under other names."

"Like what?"

"I don't know," Clint said. "You got two strangers in town?"

"Nope."

"But you had one for a while, a couple of days ago."

"Yeah, we had one, but he's gone."

"That was Dunn."

"Well, I'll be," the sheriff said. "If you knew he was here, why didn't you come and get 'im?"

"Because I found out too late," Clint said, "but I'm looking for him now—him and his friend."

"What'd they do?"

"Tried to kill me, and stole my horse."

"Then I guess I know why you're lookin' for them so hard."

"They were here," Clint said, "with a wagon, and an extra horse."

The sheriff rubbed his jaw.

"They pay you to keep quiet?"

The lawman didn't respond.

"Or did they pay you to point me toward them?" Clint asked. "Because I'm sure they're waiting for me, with some extra men."

When you accuse a lawman of taking a payoff, their reaction is always an indication of whether or not you're wrong or right. This lawman took it calmly, just staring back at Clint.

"My name is Patrick Buford," he said calmly, "and if you're gonna accuse me of takin' money, you better have some proof, son." His tone was not as laid back as his manner.

"I didn't accuse you of anything," Clint said. "I was just making a statement."

"If you're trackin' your men, then keep on trackin', friend," Buford said. "I ain't seen 'em."

Clint couldn't call him a liar until he found out what Cain had learned.

"Okay, Sheriff," Clint said. "Sorry if I offended. I didn't mean any offense."

"Well, offense taken," Buford said.

There wasn't much to say to that, so Clint turned and left the office.

Clint found the smallest saloon in town. It was so small it didn't even have a name, just a board over the door on which someone had written the word SALOON. There was also no one inside but the bartender, and Cain.

Clint entered and joined Cain at the bar.

"What'll it be?" the young bartender asked. He had a towel over his shoulder, but it was dry. It was there for appearance' sake. Clint had a feeling this was his first job in a saloon.

"Beer."

"Comin' up."

"I talked with Sheriff Buford," Clint told Cain. "I think I pretty much insulted him."

"How?"

"I may have insinuated that he'd been paid off," Clint said. "He said he hadn't seen two strangers in town."

"I don't think he has," Cain said.

The bartender put a beer in front of Clint. Cain was still working on his.

"How so?"

"I followed the tracks," Cain said. "They didn't go through town, but around."

"Why bother driving to this town, and then going around it?" Clint asked.

"That I could not read in the tracks," Cain said. "I just know that they bypassed the town."

"So we're wasting time here."

"Yes."

"Then let's get out of here," Clint said.

Cain finished his beer, while Clint drank down half of his. He paid for both, and they left.

Outside, Clint and Cain mounted their horses.

"I've got a question for you, Cain," Clint said.

Cain looked at him.

"We're following a wagon trail, with my horse trailing along behind."

"That is right."

"What about other horses?" Clint asked. "Trailing behind? Or riding alongside?"

Cain stared at him.

"Or are both men riding in the wagon?" Clint went on. "And if so, why? Why a wagon? Why aren't they on horseback?"

"You make good points," Cain said, "but some of your questions I cannot answer. All I see are the wagon and your horse. If there are two men, they have to be in the wagon. But there could only be one man."

"Which would mean the other might have ridden on ahead," Clint said.

"That figures," Cain said.

"So maybe the wagon led us here to force us to waste time."

"For what?"

"Until they get ready for us. Or for me. They probably don't know you're along."

"That could work to your benefit."

"Yes, it could," Clint said. "We can talk about how along the way."

TWENTY-SIX

Cain took Clint outside of town and showed him the trail as it circled around to the other side.

"This road is not as well traveled as the road to Hastings," the big half-breed said, pointing down. "The tracks are much easier to follow."

"That's because they want me to follow them," Clint said. "If what happened in Orwell is any indication, they're definitely waiting for me."

"And even knowing that, you are going to ride in anyway," Cain said.

"Yes."

"Well," Cain said, "maybe we can find out how many guns we will be facing."

"We?"

"Well, yes," Cain said, "you hired me to track. I figure you don't expect me to just watch while you get shot up."

"I assume you'll want some extra money to back my play."

"Of course."

"I don't have a problem with that."

Clint didn't know how proficient Cain was with a gun, but he really wasn't in a position to refuse the help.

* * *

They continued to follow the trail, stopping only briefly to spell the horses. They ate beef jerky and washed it down with water along the way.

Abruptly, Cain reined his horse in. Clint went on a few yards before he realized what had happened, and rode back.

"What happened?"

Cain pointed to the ground.

"Other horses."

"We know there are other tracks on this road."

"No," Cain said, "the wagon was joined here by riders"—he continued to point—"on both sides."

"How many?"

Cain took a moment, then said, "At least four."

"So five men altogether."

"Depending on how many are in the wagon," the half-breed reminded him.

"Right."

Cain looked at Clint.

"This does not mean there are only these men," he said. "There could be more waiting for them at their destination."

"I understand that."

"We will see if they are joined by any others along the way," Cain said.

"Apparently," Clint said, "the original two men are not willing to face me alone."

"That is obvious," Cain said, "especially since they attempted to bushwhack you."

Clint looked ahead of them.

"I wonder if they're leading us to another town."

"If they are, it is not Orwell," Cain said.

"What's up ahead?"

"Dover," Cain said, "and Hooper."

"What kind of towns?"

"Small ones."

"What else is ahead?"

"Canyons," Cain said. "Some of them have been used by gangs in the past."

"That's probably it, then," Clint said. "My bet is they're leading us to a canyon, looking to trap me."

"And bushwhack you again."

"Guess they think it was a good idea that just didn't work," Clint said.

"Cowards," Cain said.

"No doubt," Clint said. "Let's continue on and see where we end up."

"You are not going to expect me to ride into a trap with you, are you?" Cain asked.

"No," Clint said, "once we figure out where they are, we'll also figure out an approach. Nobody's riding into a trap."

"Good."

"Unless we have to . . ."

Adam Dunn came out of the shack, where Derrick Sands was waiting with their horses.

"Are we set?" Dunn asked.

"All set."

"How many men?"

"Six," Sands said. "One man on watch all the time."

"Good."

"Where are we headed?" Sands asked.

"Away from here," Dunn said. "We might head for Kerrville, send a telegram from there for instructions."

"Are we payin' these men ahead of time?"

"Half," Dunn said. "They'll get the other half when the job is done."

"And that's okay with them?"

"Hey," Dunn said, "they're just real excited about gettin' a chance to kill the Gunsmith."

"It better work this time," Sands said. "We could be runnin' out of men."

"As long as there's more money," Dunn assured him, "there'll be more men."

"If you say so," Sands said.

"I do," Dunn said. "Come on, let's ride."

TWENTY-SEVEN

As they continued to follow the trail—which pretty much stuck to the main road—they encountered the tracks of a few more men.

"How many does that make now?" Clint asked.

"If there's only one man on the wagon," Cain said, "I count eight men."

"Hopefully, there aren't more waiting for them."

"Eight to two," Cain said. "Those aren't very good odds."

"If they do it the way they did in Orwell, it'll be three to one," Clint pointed out. "Dunn and Sands probably won't be there."

"Then we will need at least one alive, to tell us where they are."

"Yes, we will."

Cain frowned.

"It's very difficult to keep someone alive when lead is flying around. We could get killed trying not to kill someone."

"Well," Clint said, "our own lives will be top priority. How's that?"

"It works well for me," Cain said.

They had already bypassed one of the small towns Cain had mentioned.

"Hooper is ahead," Cain said, "but we will come to some canyons before that."

"That's my bet," Clint said.

As they approached the canyons, Cain stopped again.

"What is it?"

"The wagon continues on toward Hooper," he said, "but the horses veer off and head for those canyons."

"And my horse?"

"He is with the tracks going towards the canyons."

"None of the men rode with the wagon?"

"No."

"They're bound to have someone on the lookout," Clint said. "We need to find which canyon they're in before they see us."

"We cannot do that on horseback."

"You want us to go on foot?"

"Not us," Cain said, "me."

"And what do you want me to do?"

"Stay with the horses," Cain said. "I will scout ahead on foot and return."

"You better."

They dismounted, walked the horses off the road until they reached a boulder Cain could sit on. He took a pair of moccasins from his saddlebags, took off his boots, and put the moccasins on.

"I will leave my rifle."

"Is that wise?"

"I will not want to make any noise," he said, "so I would not be firing it. I have my knife."

"Okay," Clint said, "you know what you're doing."

Cain looked around, then pointed.

"There is a dry wash there," he said. "If you take the horses there, you won't be seen from the road. Just in case someone comes along."

"If someone does come along," Clint said, "I'll be asking them some questions."

"That is up to you. I will be back soon."

"Good luck."

As the half-breed moved off on foot, Clint took the reins of both horses and walked them to the dry wash. He grounded the reins of both horses, then found a place to sit and took out a piece of beef jerky.

Cain spotted the lookout with no trouble, also managed to avoid him. He might have been able to get behind him and kill him, but that would sooner or later alert the others that something was wrong. He and Clint weren't yet ready to announce their arrival. But at least he now knew that they had found the men. What remained was to determine how many of them there were, and exactly where.

He bypassed the lookout, moving in his moccasined feet with remarkable silence for a man his size.

The man on lookout was completely oblivious.

In seconds, Cain found a shack in the canyon, surrounded by several men. There was one fire, with three men seated around it. With the man on lookout, that made four. He wondered how many might be in the shack.

Their horses were picketed nearby. He moved to a better vantage point and was able to count six horses.

Six men.

Clint Adams had probably been right. The bushwhackers, Dunn and Sands, weren't there. Hopefully, one of them would know where the two men went. If they managed keep one alive—and the right one, at that.

He was high above the canyon, peering over the edge at the men below. He backed away and started to make his way back to Clint.

As he passed the point where he'd seen the lookout, he noticed the man was gone. Had he been relieved? And if so, where was the new man?

He came around a turn and found out for himself. The lookout was just doing up his pants, having just relieved himself on a rock, which was steaming as a result. The two men froze when they saw each other.

The lookout had set his rifle aside to take his piss, but he was wearing a gun and holster. He went for the gun, but he was no fast draw. Cain produced his knife and was on the man before he could draw his weapon.

As shocked as he was at this giant Indian attacking him, the man managed to get a hand up to defend himself, deflecting Cain's knife. In seconds the men were locked together, but Cain's superior strength quickly asserted itself. As the knife pierced the lookout's chest, he opened his mouth to scream. Cain clamped his other hand over the man's mouth to muffled the yell, and then the body went limp and he lowered it to the ground.

He pulled the body out of sight behind the piss rock and then rushed to join Clint. Now that he'd killed one man, they didn't have much time.

TWENTY-EIGHT

Clint looked up as Cain was coming back. He hadn't heard him, but sensed him. He stood up.

"What's up? You look like you're in a hurry."

"I am," Cain said. "There were six men in the canyon, but now there are five."

"What happened?"

Cain told him how he'd encountered the lookout as he was relieving himself, and had to kill him to keep him quiet.

"Then we better move before they send somebody to relieve him," Clint said.

They paused, stared at each other, then decided that the double use of the word "relieve" was not a joke. Nobody laughed.

"Let's move," Cain said, picking up his rifle.

Clint removed his rifle from his saddle, and followed the big man.

They passed the rock Cain had hidden the dead man behind and Cain pointed.

"He was up there," he said, pointing up.

"Well, nobody's there now," Clint said, "which is lucky."

"The rest are over here," Cain said.

"Lead the way."

They both eased up to the edge and looked down into the canyon.

"Five," Clint said. "Any in the shack?"

"I don't think so," Cain said. "See? Only six horses."

"Right."

As they watched, the five men sitting around the fire broke out a bottle of whiskey.

"We could wait for them to get drunk," Cain proposed.

"But if they start to send someone to spell the other one as lookout, we'd have to move fast. No, let's just move in and take them as quickly as possible."

"All right."

Clint looked around, looked at the six horses.

"Where's Eclipse?"

"What?"

"My horse. Where is he?"

"I don't see him."

"No, I don't either," Clint said. "That's why I'm asking."

"Maybe he's in the shack?"

"Damn it!" Clint swore. "If he's not here . . ."

"Why don't we just ask them?" Cain said.

Clint firmed his jaw, then said, "Yes, why don't we. How good are you with that rifle?"

"I would not be able to hit anyone from here," Cain said. "Not with my first shot anyway."

"All right, then," Clint sad, "let's move in closer."

They circled around so they could come at the men from behind the shack.

"I want to get a look inside first," Clint said, "to see if Eclipse is in there."

"All right."

They moved to the back wall of the shack. It wasn't built well, and there was space between the slats that made up the wall. Clint peered in, moved, peered in again, then said, "No, he's not in there." He looked at Cain. "He's not here."

"And neither are Dunn and Sands, we assume," Cain said. "So they probably have your horse with them."

"I hope he's taken a piece out of each of them," Clint said angrily.

"Should we take these fellas?" Cain asked.

"Yes," Clint said. "Circle around to that side. Count to ten. Got it?"

"Got it."

Cain split off from Clint, and they moved around the shack, counting.

Around the fire, Sam Roosevelt said, "Somebody's got to go and spell Clay."

"Whose turn is it?" Andy Gunner asked. He was a big fellow in his thirties who was dumb as a stump and always the butt of the others' jokes.

"Yours," Doug Smythe said. He was a bespectacled, sandy-haired man whose benign appearance masked his toughness.

"I don't think so," Gunner said.

"Yeah, it is," Bill Wade said with a big smile.

Gunner couldn't argue, because he couldn't remember for sure if it was his turn or not.

As Gunner started to get to his feet, Clint Adams stepped out into the open . . .

"Everybody just take it easy!" Clint called.

They all turned and stared. Gunner was the only one on his feet, and he did what his gut told him to do. He went for his gun.

Clint drew and fired. The bullet hit Gunner in the mid-section and folded him up.

Cain fired, too, and despite what he'd told Clint, his first bullet hit Gunner.

The others, realizing they were in a cross fire, reacted badly. They all jumped to their feet, going for their guns.

"Damn it!" Clint swore. As the four men leveled their guns to fire, he doubted he and Cain would be able to keep any of them alive.

He was right.

TWENTY-NINE

Afterward, Clint and Cain walked among the bodies.

"All dead," Cain said.

"I know, damn it."

"I'll walk the area, see what I can find," Cain said.

"Yeah, okay."

Clint was upset that they'd killed six men and hadn't learned anything about Eclipse. He moved among the dead, checking pockets. He found money, but nothing that would tell him where his horse had been taken. He went through their saddlebags with the same result. More money and a couple of letters, but they were personal and not helpful to the situation.

He walked over to Cain, who was looking off into the distance.

"What have you got?" he asked.

"Tracks," the half-breed said, "leading off that way."

Clint looked in that direction and saw only canyon walls.

"How many?" he asked.

"Three," Cain said. "Two saddle mounts"—he looked at Clint—"and your horse. He was in the shack at one time."

"What the hell is that way?" Clint wondered aloud.

"Let's find out," Cain said.

"Okay," Clint said, "but first I want to let their horses go free."

Cain nodded.

Clint went to where the horses were picketed and released them all. They milled about, but Clint knew that sooner or later they'd go in search of some water.

"Okay," Clint said. "Let's go."

Cain set off on foot with Clint right behind him. The tracks just seemed to be taking them toward a solid wall, but before long it became obvious.

"See that?" Cain asked.

"Looks like a fissure."

Cain looked at Clint.

"There's a way out here," the half-breed said. "The box canyon is not such a box."

They continued on, finally coming to the opening.

"Wide enough for horses," Cain said, looking in.

"Then we need our mounts," Clint said.

They had to walk out of the canyon, get their horses, and come back in. To do that they had to pass the bodies twice. Cain finally asked the question.

"Do we want to bury these men?"

"No," Clint said. "I found enough money in their pockets to tell me they were hired to kill me. Let the buzzards have them."

Cain shrugged. It didn't matter to him.

They rode their horses to the fissure, then dismounted.

"We'll walk them through," Cain suggested.

"No argument from me."

The opening went all the way to the top, so there was some light as they went along. Cain stopped and pointed to the wall. There was a splotch of red.

"Blood," he said. "It looks like you got your wish."

"Good boy," Clint said, thinking of Eclipse talking bite out of one of the men. He only hoped they didn't punish the horse for it.

As they continued to walk their mounts, the fissure narrowed, widened, twisted, and turned, but eventually they came out the other side.

"Where are we?" Clint asked.

"Let's ride a bit and I will get my bearings," Cain said.

They mounted up and Cain continued to follow the tracks.

"All right," he said, "I have it now. These tracks are heading for Hooper."

"How big a town?"

"Not big," Cain said. "No telegraph."

"Law?"

"A sheriff."

"Any good?"

"I do not know him."

"Been there?"

"Once or twice."

"What kind of town?"

Cain thought a moment, then said, "Sleepy."

"Not wide open?"

"No."

"Then why are they going there?"

"We do know one thing," Cain said.

"What?"

"Even if they thought you might not be killed in that canyon," Cain said, "they would not expect you to find the back way out through that fissure."

"So they're not leading me to Hooper deliberately."

"No."

"They might be there when we get there," Clint said.

"They might."

"How far behind are we?"

Cain studied the ground.

"I would say they passed this way this morning," Cain said. "They are about six hours ahead of us."

Clint scowled.

"They could have been there and gone by now," he said.

"They must have had plans for the men in the canyon to contact them, let them know you were dead."

"They'd need a telegraph for that."

"After they killed you, the men could have ridden back to Dover to use the telegraph."

"Yes," Clint said, "but where would they send it to?"

"After Dover," Cain said, "is Kerrville."

"They would have a telegraph."

"Yes, they would."

"All right," Clint said, "let's keep to the tracks and see where they take us."

THIRTY

The trail led to Hooper.

"Right into town," Cain said.

"And leading Eclipse behind them," Clint said. "Nobody can say they didn't notice them this time."

It was dusk when they rode in. They'd have to stay the night, get an easy start in the morning. Neither of them believed there was any chance that Dunn and Sands—and Eclipse—were still in town. They confirmed this with the old gent who ran the livery.

"Yeah, they rode in leading that beautiful Arabian," he said. "I offered a good price to buy him, but they said they had plans for him. Plans." He almost spit. "Them two wouldn't know what to do with good horseflesh."

"Had one of them been bitten?" Clint asked.

The man closed one eye and regarded Clint quizzically.

"How did you know that?" Then he asked, "Say, is that your horse?"

"It is."

"I knew them fellers stole it."

"How long did they stay?"

"Not long," he said. "Didn't even unsaddle their mounts.

Just asked me to feed the three and they came back for them in, oh, 'bout an hour. Then they was off again."

"Was he all right?" Clint asked.

"He was in fine fettle," the man said. "Good-lookin' animal, that one. I watered and fed the three. He waren't no trouble a'tall."

"You know which way they headed?" Cain asked.

"Didn't see," the man said, "but from what I heard, I'd say they went toward Kerrville."

"Much obliged," Clint said. "We'll be leaving early in the morning to keep tracking them."

"Say, this steeldust is kinda nice," the man said. "You wanna sell 'im?"

"He's not mine to sell," Clint said. "I'm just using him until I get my horse back."

"Been trackin' them long?"

"Not long. But I'll track them as long as I have to, to get him back," Clint said.

"See?" the man said. "Now that's the way a fella is supposed ta feel about his horse."

They left the livery and went to the town's one hotel. The clerk didn't look happy about giving a room to a half-breed, but he didn't comment. Clint felt he was intimidated by Cain's size, and would not have dared refuse him.

They went to their rooms and dumped their gear, then met back in the lobby again.

"Sheriff's office?" Cain asked.

"Steak first," Clint said.

"Suits me," the big man said.

"Where can we get a decent steak?" Clint asked the young desk clerk.

"San Antone, Waco, Fort Worth," the man said. "If you mean in this town, though, the best one you're gonna find will be across the street and up a ways. Bob's Café. He'll likely burn it, but it'll be edible."

"Well," Clint said, "I guess I'm hungry enough to eat it well done."

They left the hotel and walked to the café.

"Burnt?" Cain asked, making a face.

"We'll ask the cook not to burn it so much," Clint said, "see what that gets us."

It didn't matter. Both of their steaks came well done. Almost burnt. But the potatoes and onions were good.

"Anything else, sir?" the waiter asked when they were finished.

"Yes," Clint said, "who's your sheriff?"

"His name's Bunyon, sir."

"Bunyon?" Cain repeated.

"Yes, sir."

"What's he like?" Clint asked.

The waiter, an older man in his sixties, shrugged and said, "He's all right."

"How long has he been sheriff?"

"Got elected last year," the man said, then added, "I mean, reelected, He's been sheriff a few years."

"Okay, thanks." Clint paid the bill.

"Do you want to bother talking to the sheriff?" Cain asked. "We already know they were here and gone."

"I guess not," Clint said. "I think I've met enough sheriffs lately."

Clint and Cain walked from the hotel and stopped in front of the café. They looked over the street, which was quiet. Or sleepy, as Cain had said.

"Do you feel like we're being watched?" he asked Cain, still looking around. Up and down the street. Rooftops. Windows. Doorways.

"No."

"Good," Clint said. "Neither do I."

"They left six men behind and probably expected you to be alone," Cain said. "They probably think you're dead."

"Then why keep Eclipse?"

"To hedge their bet," Cain said, "just in case."

"I suppose," Clint said. "Do you want to get a drink?"

"Yes."

Clint looked up and down the street.

"One hotel, one café, one saloon."

"Like I said," Cain replied, "a sleepy little town."

"Yeah," Clint said. "Come on, we'll have one drink. I want to get an early start tomorrow. I want this to end. And I want my goddamn horse back."

THIRTY-ONE

They had a drink in the saloon, where they were watched warily the entire time by the other patrons. However, Clint knew they were being watched because of Cain's sheer size and appearance. He looked like a man who would tear you apart with his bare hands just as soon as look at you.

They had one beer each, and then left.

"That didn't bother you?" Cain asked.

Clint knew what he was referring to.

"Are you kidding?" he said. "I was glad to have you around, have them look at you instead of me for a change."

"That's right," Cain said, "you are the Gunsmith. You have probably been stared at longer than I have."

"Well, not from birth," Clint said.

"But you are older than I am."

"Okay," Clint said, "I'll concede both points."

They walked to the hotel without incident, past the clerk—who nodded to them—and up to their floor.

"Still don't think we're being watched?" Clint asked.

"No."

"Me neither," Clint said, "but we can't be too careful."

They went to the door of Cain's room and opened it

quickly. It was empty. They then did the same thing with Clint's room, and got the same result.

Then they turned in for the night.

Early the next morning they met in the lobby. The same clerk was there, looking sleepy. He had either just gotten up, or hadn't been to sleep yet.

When they got to the livery, their horses were saddled and waiting for them.

"You said you'd be leavin' early," the man reminded them.

Clint paid him and they mounted up.

"I hope you find your horse," the liveryman said.

"So do I," Clint responded.

They rode out of town, and the big half-breed picked up their trail again.

"Still two horses, leading one—yours. And he's moving well."

"You can tell that?"

"I would be able to tell if he was limping."

"That's good to know."

They continued on.

Derrick Sands entered the saloon and sat down across from Adam Dunn.

"Nothin'?" Dunn asked.

"No telegram."

"Jesus Christ," Dunn said, shaking his head, "money can't buy good help, can it?"

"So what do we do now?"

"Well, we still have his horse."

"So?"

Dunn looked across at his colleague.

"We'll have to kill him ourselves."

"We tried that, remember?" Sands asked. "Larry got killed and we ran."

"No more runnin' this time."

"So what do we do? Ambush him again?"

"Yeah," Dunn said, "but remember, this time we have somethin' he wants."

"So how do we get him here?"

"I think we just have to wait," Dunn said. "He'll track us right here."

"And we're just gonna wait?"

"We're gonna wait," Dunn said, "and send a telegram."

Cain stopped, and Clint reined in beside him. Up ahead of them was a town.

"Kerrville," Cain said.

"Been here before?" Clint asked.

"Passed through once. You?"

"Nope. First time."

"How do you want to do this?" Cain asked. "Ride right down Main Street?"

"Not me," Clint said. "You."

Clint decided that Cain should ride into town alone. Yes, he'd attract attention, but that was only because of who he was and what he looked like. Neither Dunn nor Sands would suspect that he was riding with Clint Adams. They arranged to meet later at a hotel in town. Clint told Cain to get a room in the largest one, if there was, indeed, more than one hotel.

Clint had to slip into town another way. It was too early, though, for him to wait until after dark. That would waste a lot of the day that was left.

Kerrville was a lot larger than either Hooper, or Kirby, or even Orwell, probably even larger than Hastings. There were any number of other points of entry he could use other than the main street. Getting into town unseen would not be a problem, especially if he did it while Cain was riding in and most of the town's eyes were on him.

So he waited until Cain and his Appaloosa were almost in town before riding around to find another way in.

THIRTY-TWO

Cain rode into town, attracting at least as much attention as he usually did. He and his Appaloosa made an arresting sight together.

Clint managed to work his way around the center of town, and he ended up behind a large, two-story building, hoping that it was a hotel. It turned out he was right. He tied off the steeldust, then walked around to the front and entered. Cain's horse was secured out front, so it was no surprise to find the half-breed in the lobby.

The desk clerk, a meek little man in his forties, was watching Cain with wide eyes, as if he expected the half-breed to suddenly produce a tomahawk and start cutting people down. There were a few men and a couple of ladies in the lobby who were skirting around the big man, who was simply standing in the center of the floor.

"Where is your horse?" Cain asked Clint.

"Out back. He can stay there awhile."

"Do you want to get a room?"

"Let's find out if Dunn and Sands are here first." He approached the clerk.

"Y-Yes, sir?"

"I'm looking for two friends of mine named Dunn and Sands. Are they registered?"

The clerk looked at the register, then said, "N-No, sir, they're not registered here."

"How many other hotels in town?"

"Three," the man said.

"And boardinghouses?"

"Yes, sir, two."

"Good," Clint said, "tell me where they all are . . ."

They stepped outside the hotel, to the relief of the desk clerk.

"In Hastings, Sands stayed in a boardinghouse," Clint said. "Let's try those first."

"What about the sheriff?"

"Let's try this ourselves first," Clint said. "The fewer people we include, the better."

"Up to you," Cain said.

"I'll walk ahead," Clint said. "You'll keep the attention off me by walking alone."

"All right."

"Try to look mean," Clint said, and walked ahead before Cain could respond.

Derrick Sands was standing at the batwing doors of the Tall Texas Saloon.

"Anythin'?" Dunn asked when Sands came back to the table.

"Big half-breed rode into town," Sands said, sitting down, "but that's all."

"Alone?"

"Yeah."

"Know him?"

"Why should I?"

"Maybe you seen him in Hastings?"

Sands shook his head. "Never did."

"Go and check on the horse."

"Check for what?"

"Just make sure it's still where we put it," Dunn said, "and it's okay."

Sands held up his bandaged left hand and said, "Ya want me to let him take another hunk outta me?"

"Just be careful with him," Dunn said.

"Say," Sands said, "you ain't thinkin' of keepin' that horse, are ya?"

"Once Adams is dead, what's the difference?"

"We wuz talkin' about the good price we could get for him," Sands reminded him.

"Don't worry about it, Sands," Dunn said. "You're gonna get paid enough for this job."

"What's this feller got against the Gunsmith anyway?" Sands asked.

"I didn't ask," Dunn said, "but maybe Adams killed somebody close to him. It don't matter. We're gettin' paid to do a job."

"Yeah, yeah," Sands said, standing up. "I'll go check on that big devil."

Devil, Dunn thought. Maybe when Adams was dead, he'd change the horse's name.

When Clint reached the first boardinghouse, he waited for Cain to catch up. The lady who answered the door was obviously frightened by the big half-breed. She answered their questions—no boarders by those names or descriptions—very quickly and slammed the door in their faces.

"Maybe at the next one," Cain said, "I should just stand back."

"I agree," Clint said.

"Also," Cain said, "I think we will want to check the whorehouses."

"Good point," Clint said. "Why don't we split up? Whores are used to men of all sizes and shapes. I don't think you'll scare them. You'll probably interest them."

"Well," Cain admitted, "whores interest me."

"I'll check the other boardinghouse, and the hotels, and meet you back at the first hotel where we left our horses."

Cain nodded his agreement.

"If you find them, don't brace them," Clint said. "Just come and find me."

"Don't worry," Cain said, "I won't rob you of the pleasure of killing them yourself."

"Thanks," Clint said.

They split up from here.

THIRTY-THREE

Clint walked away from the second boardinghouse, having gotten the same answers he'd gotten at the first one, this time without having a door slammed in his face.

If Dunn and Sands were not waiting for him, they would be registered somewhere. If not a boardinghouse, then a hotel. But if, by now, they assumed Clint had not been killed, and they were expecting him, would they be hiding? Or would they position themselves where he could see them?

Like in a saloon?

He decided to check the other hotels before going to the saloons.

Cain walked into the town's one whorehouse, and some of the girls were immediately drawn to him.

"You're lookin' for me, honey," a blonde said.

"I'm the one you want, baby," a brunette said.

"Like redheads, honey?" a third asked.

Cain would have liked to take all three upstairs with him, but before he could say anything, an older woman spilling out of her nightgown came up behind the girls and clapped her hands. The flesh of her arms jiggled as she did it.

"Now, girls," she said, "you know we don't crowd the

customers as they come in. Get into the parlor with the others."

The three girls all whispered their names to him before they obeyed.

"You're a big one," she said to Cain. "My girls are gonna have to work hard to satisfy you."

"I am looking for two men."

"That's disappointing. Sorry, honey," she said, "we only have girls here, no men."

"I mean," he said, "I am trying to find two men who may have come here."

"Friends of yours?"

"Yes," he said, "they are called—"

She waved him off and said, "I don't bother with names myself. Maybe one of the girls will know. But you can describe them to me."

He did, giving her the descriptions Clint had given him.

"That could be anybody," she said. "Why don't you go into the parlor, talk to some of the girls, and then maybe pick one or two that you like and take them upstairs?"

"I will talk to them."

He went into the parlor and the girls mobbed him again. They were all powdered and perfumed and falling out of their nighties, and his head swam with the scent of them and the sight of their smooth skin.

But he wasn't there to enjoy their charms. He picked out two or three, took them to a sofa with them, and asked his questions.

Clint tried the hotels with no luck and wondered what was taking Cain so long. Maybe he'd found a girl or two he liked and decided to sample their wares? Clint doubted the big half-breed would do that before they were finished with their hunt.

After the boardinghouses and the hotels, Clint had the saloons left. But walking into a saloon might be walking right into a trap. If he'd learned nothing else in Orwell, he had learned that.

He decided to check the livery stables instead, see if anyone had laid eyes on Eclipse. That was something people would remember.

Cain sat with one girl in his lap, and one on either side of him. The little redhead in his lap was rubbing her butt against the huge bulge in his pants, all excited. The other girls were letting their breasts loose from their nightgowns, rubbing them on his arms and chest, or placing them in his big hands.

The usually stolid half-breed was sweating. He had a weakness for women—preferably young ones with red or blond hair, and two of these qualified.

"Come on, honey," the redhead said into his ear, while squirming around in his lap, rubbing him with her neat little bottom. "Take me upstairs and ride me hard."

"Another time," he said.

"Soon?" she asked.

"I promise," he said. "Very soon."

"Me, too?" the blonde asked.

"Yes, you, too."

The brunette had sensed his lack of interest in her and had slipped away.

"But tell me, have either of you seen the men I'm talking about?"

The little blonde frowned.

"What are their names again?"

"Dunn and Sands."

"Sands," the redhead said. "I think Molly said somethin' about two fellas who came in. Maybe she knows."

"Which one is Molly?"

"You relax, honey," the blonde said. "I'll get 'er."

As the blonde slipped away from them, the redhead slid her hand into his crotch and grabbed him.

"Oh, my God," she said, "are you sure—"

"Yes," he said, "believe me, I am sure."

She stroked him, kissed his neck, and said, "Too bad. I ain't never been with a man as big as you."

"I promise," he said, his mouth very dry, "soon."

"I seen a horse like that."

Clint was talking to a man who worked in a small livery stable near the hotel.

"When?"

The man rubbed his jaw and said, "Earlier today. I remember wishing they had brought it here to me."

"Where did you see it?"

"Somewhere in town," the old man said. He took off his hat and scratched his balding head. "My memory ain't as good as it used to be. Maybe it was last week?"

"Look," Clint said, "just relax and think, old-timer. This is important. Where did you see that horse?"

The blonde brought Molly over, a young and energetic girl with short, dark hair.

"This is Molly."

"Wow, big boy," she said, "you can handle the three of us, can't you?"

"I will," he said, "I will come back and do that. These girls told me you saw the two men I'm looking for."

"What men?"

"Sands and Dunn."

She frowned.

"What do they look like?"

He described them while struggling against the redhead's groping hand.

"I did see them," Molly said. "In fact, one of them took me upstairs."

Cain put his hands under the redhead's butt, lifted her off his lap, and set her aside.

"Tell me," he said to Molly, "when."

THIRTY-FOUR

Clint got to the hotel lobby first. Rather than standing in the center the way Cain did, he took a seat against the wall to wait.

Cain came walking in several minutes later and joined Clint, who now understood why the big man had been standing earlier. The furniture in the lobby was too flimsy to hold his bulk.

"I think I found Eclipse," Clint said.

"I think I found Dunn and Sands," Cain said.

Clint looked around the lobby. Once again they were the center of attention.

"Let's get rooms so we can talk without being watched," Clint suggested.

"All right."

Clint went to the desk to register for the two of them. He used phony names and collected two keys from the clerk. They then went up to one of the rooms, where they could sit and discuss what they had each discovered.

"You first," Clint said.

"Both Dunn and Sands went to the whorehouse earlier today," Cain said. "One of the girls—her name is Molly—remembered. She went upstairs with Sands. She doesn't remember who went upstairs with the other man, but she's trying to find out."

"Does she know where they were staying?" Clint asked.

"She got the impression they were staying with someone, and not in any of the hotels."

"That explains why they're not registered anywhere."

"What about your horse?"

"I found an old-timer in the livery who says he saw Eclipse earlier today. At least, he thinks it was earlier today."

"He doesn't know?"

"His memory is a little fuzzy," Clint said.

"Where did he see him?"

"That's also something he's trying to remember."

"What can we do to help his memory?"

"I'm thinking money, whiskey, or both," Clint said. "I wanted to come back here and talk to you. I told him I'd be back."

"That is what I told the ladies."

"Was it tough on you?" Clint asked.

"You don't know," Cain said. "I like whores."

"Would you rather I go back?"

"No, that's all right," the half-breed said. "I do not mind going back."

"Maybe, when this is all done, you can go back for a while," Clint said.

"I promised them I would," Cain said. "And I always keep my promises."

"I'm sure that'll make them very happy," Clint said. "Let's go see if we can get some definite answers."

"Do you think he'd really come walkin' in here?" Derrick Sands asked.

"Why not?" Dunn asked. "Comin' in off the trail, he'll want a drink."

"Yeah," Sands said, scowling, "but won't he figure on us bein' here?"

"Sure, and he'll figure he can handle us," Dunn said. "After all, he's the Gunsmith."

"Well, yeah," Sands said worriedly, "I been thinkin' about that, too."

"What?"

"We've left five men and six men to kill him now," Sands said, "and we tried ourselves. Ain't nothin' worked. What makes you think the two of us can do it?"

"We've got somethin' they didn't have."

"His horse?"

"That's right," Dunn said. "He ain't gonna do a thing while we got that animal."

"He ain't gonna get killed for it!" Sands argued.

"I guess we'll just have to wait and see how right you are, Derrick," Dunn said.

Sands frowned, still not convinced.

"Relax," Dunn said, "and go to the bar and get us another bottle of whiskey."

THIRTY-FIVE

When Clint returned to the livery stable, he had managed to wrangle a bottle of whiskey out of the desk clerk at the hotel. The old man's rheumy eyes brightened when he saw the bottle.

"That might jog my memory," he admitted. "Yep, sure might." He licked his lips.

Clint unstoppered the bottle, handed it over, let the old man take a healthy swig, and then took it away from him.

The old man wiped his mouth with the back of his hand.

"All right," Clint said, "think about it. Where'd you see that horse?"

"Big feller, right?"

"That's right."

"White over here," he said, touching his own nose.

"Yes." There was a white crescent on his nose, which was why Clint had called him Eclipse.

"Hmm, yeah," the old man said, frowning, "I seen him . . . somewhere."

He looked at the whiskey bottle and Clint let him have another drink.

"Okay," Clint said, "how about this? Let's go over what you did this morning, and maybe it'll come back to you."

"Kin we take the bottle with us?"

"Sure," Clint said, "we'll take the bottle with us. What's the first thing you did this morning . . ."

"I ain't gonna tell you," Molly said to Cain.

"What?"

She leaned into him and said, "I ain't gonna tell ya."

"Why not?"

"I want somethin'."

"What?"

"Come upstairs with me," she said. "I wanna see you."

"Huh?"

"I wanna see you with no pants on."

"Now look—"

"You ain't so scary, you know," she said, leaning into him as they sat on the sofa together. She wasn't his type, but he couldn't take his eyes off her full breasts as she pressed them together. They swelled and threatened to come out. "Come upstairs with me, and I'll tell you what I know."

"Promise?" he asked.

"I promise," she said.

"Well . . . okay." He thought this might be better then spending time arguing with her, or threatening.

They got dirty looks from the other girls as she took his hand and led him up the stairs.

The old man lived in a shack at the edge of town. He walked Clint there.

"There ya go," he said, waving. "I woke up and walked into town."

"Okay, let's do it," Clint said. "Make sure you take the same route."

"I walk the same way every day," the old man insisted.

"Good," Clint said, "then you'll remember."

The old man eyed the bottle.

"I'd remember better if I could wet my whistle a bit."

"I'm gonna give you one more sip," Clint told him. "After that you can have the rest of the bottle, but only if you tell me where you saw my horse."

"Your horse?" the old man asked.

"That's right."

"You mean them fellers stole yore horse?"

"That's right."

"Sonsofbitches!" the old man swore.

Clint handed him the bottle and watched while he took a swig, then grabbed it.

"Let's get 'em!" the old man said.

Clint hoped the old coot could hold his liquor and wasn't already drunk.

"Which way?" he asked.

"This-a-way . . ."

Cain let the girl drag him down the hall to a door, waited while she opened it. Then she got behind him and pushed him in, slamming the door behind them.

"Those other girls hate me now," she said.

He thought about the blonde and the redhead, but when Molly turned to face him and dropped her nightgown to the floor, he forgot about them. She was medium height, with full breasts, wide hips, and a generous butt. Between her legs was a forest of brown hair. He always liked when a girl had a big bush. He could already smell that she was ready, and he was about to burst from his pants.

"You like?" she asked, putting her hands on her hips.

He stared at her hardening brown nipples and said, "Yeah, I like."

"Okay, then," she said, "your turn."

"Okay," he said, "I really got to go, Molly, so you just want me to take off my pants so you can look, right?"

"Right."

"And then you'll tell me what I want to know, right?"

"Right. Come on, don't keep me waiting, honey," she said anxiously.

Cain set his rifle aside, then his knife, then undid his trousers and pulled them down. He didn't wear any underwear. His penis sprang out from his crotch.

"Oh . . . my . . . God!" she breathed.

THIRTY-SIX

Clint followed the liveryman toward town, hoping the old coot was taking the same route, hoping against hope that seeing a big horse with a white blaze wasn't just some dream he'd had.

"I stopped here and waved to old Mrs. Cartwright," the geezer said. "She called out, 'Hi, Jake,' and I said—"

"That's okay, Jake," Clint said. "I don't need to know everything you said. Where'd you go from here?"

Jake turned and stared at the whiskey bottle.

"No more," Clint said. "Not until you show me where you saw my horse."

"Okay," the old man said reluctantly, "well, then I went this-a-way . . ."

Molly put her hands over her mouth and stared at Cain's erect penis. It was easily the biggest and prettiest one she'd ever seen.

"I ain't never seen a tallywacker like that before," she told him.

"Okay," he said, starting to reach for his pants, but she leaped forward and block his hands.

"I wanna touch it," she said.

"But you said—"

"I know, but geez, look at it," she said. "You can't expect me not to touch it."

He swore to himself that he wouldn't tell Clint that this happened.

"Yeah, okay," he said, dropping his hands to his sides.

"Okay," she said, "okay."

She got down on her knees.

Jake took Clint through a neighborhood of large homes that made him think it was a mistake. What reason would the old man have to walk by any of these homes?

"Jake," Clint said, "are you sure—"

"I always stop at Mr. Everett's house to see if he needs any work done," the old man said.

"Oh, I see. And did he?"

"No," Jake said, "then I usually stop at Mr. Clement's house for the same reason."

"And did he need work done?"

"No," Jake said, "and he got mad at me, told me to get away from the house. He never did that before."

"Why did he do that?"

"I don't know," Jake said, "but I was curious. So I went around to the back of the house . . ."

"Jake?"

The old man turned, pointed at the bottle of whiskey, and exclaimed, "That's mine!"

"Why?"

"Because that's where I saw your horse," the old man said. "Behind Mr. Clement's house!"

Molly got to her knees in front of Cain and took his huge penis in both of her hands. She held it as if it were a club.

"Oh my God," she said again. She didn't know what was more incredible, its length or its girth.

"Molly—"

"Shh," she said. She touched the spongy head with her fingertips, then ran them underneath. He jumped and his cock jerked.

"Oh my . . ." she said.

"Molly . . ."

"Shh," she said again. She leaned forward and licked the head of his cock.

"I don't know if I can get this in my mouth, but . . ." She leaned forward again and this time wrapped her lips around him, and took him in.

"Molly . . ." he said for a third time, but this time he had no intention of trying to stop her. Instead, he reached down and put his hands on her head, which began to bob up and down on him.

The wetter she got his cock, the more of it she was able to get into her mouth. She reached down and cradled his heavy ball sack in one hand. She continued to suck him, making sounds that were a cross between gulping and gagging.

She pulled her head back and released him, gasped as she tried to catch her breath.

"My God."

He reached down to take her breasts in his hands. With his thumbs, he strummed her nipples.

"Do you want me to stop?" she asked. "And let you leave?"

"Don't be stupid," he said. He reached down, put his hands in her armpits. Holding her that way, he lifted her up and carried her to the bed.

"Come on, come on," she urged him. "I want that monster inside me."

He pulled off his shirt, staggered around until he got his boots off, and kicked his trousers away from his ankles.

"Jesus," she said, "look at the size of you! You're big all over, ain't you?"

"I am," he said, "but only one place counts right now."

He got on the bed with her, spread her legs, and reached into her bush. His fingers found her wet and ready.

"Yeah, see, I'm ready," she said. "Come on. But go slow at first. You're liable to tear me up. I've never had one this big before."

He ran his hands over her smooth flesh, leaned over to first bite and suck her nipples before he turned his attention back to her crotch.

He pressed the bulbous head of his penis to her pussy lips, rubbed it up and down until he was wet, then started to slide it in.

"Ooh, ooh, ooh . . ." she said.

"Are you all right?" he asked.

She reached up to put her hands on his arms.

"I'm fine," she said. "Keep going."

He did, sliding himself into her farther. She brought her legs up, wrapped them around his waist. As he pushed in as far as he could, she closed her eyes and bit her lip. However, she didn't try to stop him, so he started moving in and out of her.

"Oh, wow," she gasped, "oh, geez." She began to move with him, her hips matching his tempo. "Ooh, yeah, that's good, that's soooo good . . ."

He put his hands on the bed on either side of her and leaned over her, keeping his weight off her.

"Mmmm," she moaned, "yes . . ."

He started to grunt as he fucked her. She tightened her legs around him, her thighs surprisingly strong.

"Come on," she said, "you can go harder . . . go faster . . . go ahead, tear me up."

He began to move faster, his giant cock glistening with her juices as he slid in and out of her. Then the door opened and suddenly they were joined on the bed by two more naked girls.

"You promised . . ." the redhead said into his ear, sliding

her hand along the crack of his butt. She rubbed her bare tits and hard nipples over his skin.

The blonde kissed his neck and slid her hand beneath him to stroke his balls. He almost exploded at her touch.

He closed his eyes and thought about the great spirit.

THIRTY-SEVEN

Clint had Jake show him where Mr. Clement's house was.

"Okay," he said, handing the old man the whiskey bottle, "you can go."

"Thanks, mister," Jake said. "I hope you get your horse back."

"Don't worry," Clint said, "I will."

Jake scurried off to finish his bottle, hugging it close to his body.

Clint stared at the two-story house, with four white pillars in front. If Jake hadn't been completely drunk and had remembered accurately, Eclipse might be behind it. Also, Dunn and Sands might be inside.

He had told Cain not to do anything until they were together, but he felt that he had to determine whether or not Eclipse was actually there.

He looked around. The area was very quiet, with no foot traffic. People would probably start returning home from work, but he still had some time before that happened.

There was a fence around the front of the house, but rather than opening the gate—many gates squeaked—he skirted the fence to get to the side of the house, then moved along the wall to the back.

He peered around to see if anyone was there. The only thing he saw was what looked like a carriage house—something you usually found in the East, not the West.

Keeping an eye on the house, he made his way to the carriage house. The door was locked. He might have gotten in by shooting the lock, but that would have alerted whoever was in the house. He moved to the side of the building 'til he found a window, and looked in.

And there he was.

Eclipse.

"Hey, big boy," Clint said to himself. The horse looked all right. He was tied, but he had a feed bin nearby and didn't look any worse for wear.

At least Clint knew the horse was safe.

Keeping a wary eye on the house, he made his way back to the street, hopefully without having been seen from the inside.

Cain left the whorehouse on weakened legs. Those whores would not let him out of that room—hell, out of that bed—until they had each sampled what was between his legs. And then they wanted to be paid! Well, he paid them, and then got the information Molly had promised him. He remembered with a sigh just how he got it . . .

"I heard them talkin' about a house they were stayin' at in the high-priced part of town," Molly said.

"That's it?" Cain asked.

She shrugged, which made her breasts jiggle, and said, "That's all I heard."

She was lying on the bed, naked, her limbs entwined with those of her naked girlfriends. Her flesh was darker, while the blonde was pale and the redhead freckled. Seeing the three naked women there, he couldn't get mad. At least Molly had given them a place to look, even if her information was kind of spare.

"Are you gonna come back, honey?" the redhead asked.

"If I can," he said, "before I have to leave town."

"You got to come back, spend more time," the blonde said.

"Come on," Molly said, "promise."

"No," he said, "I will not promise!"

"Don't be mad," Molly told him with a pout. "I told you what I know."

"Yeah, you did," he said.

She smiled at him and said, "You didn't really think all I wanted to do was look, did you?"

The three girls were laughing as he went out the door . . .

Now, on the street, Cain made his way back to the hotel to meet with Clint.

The girl Molly had bamboozled him, and got him to her room upstairs. She got him into bed so the other girls could come in later. He couldn't be mad because three whores wanted to get him into bed. But while he had a grin on his face as he walked away, this sure wasn't something he was going to tell Clint Adams about.

THIRTY-EIGHT

This time, instead of waiting for Cain in the lobby, Clint waited in his room. He left the door unlocked, and Cain walked right in.

"Got it," he said. "A big house somewhere in town—"

"I know," Clint said. "I found it."

"A house?" Cain asked. "A rich man's house?"

Clint nodded and said, "I saw Eclipse. He's locked in a carriage house in the back."

"What about the two men?"

"I didn't see them," Clint said. "They might have been in the house."

"So what do we do now?" Cain asked. "Go to the house and knock on the door?"

"We don't know what we'd be walking into," Clint said. "They think they have the upper hand because they have Eclipse."

"Then," Cain said, "let's go and take your horse back."

"My thought exactly."

"It's gonna be dark soon," Sands said to Dunn.

"So?"

"I don't think he's comin' 'til maybe tomorrow."

"He might already be in town," Dunn said.

"You think he slipped in without us seein' him?" Sands asked. "We been watchin' the street."

"He didn't have to use the street," Dunn said. "There are other ways to get into town."

"Then what do we do?"

"We get ready," Dunn said.

"Back at the house?"

"Yeah," Dunn said. "We better dig in."

"How will we know if he's here?"

"We'll have Clement send some men out to find out," Dunn said.

"He's gonna have to pay 'em."

"He's got men workin' for him already," Dunn said. "Don't worry. We'll find out if Adams is in town." Dunn finished his drink and said, "Let's go."

They left the saloon, where they had been sitting all day long. As they went out the door, the bartender breathed a sigh of relief.

"After dark," Clint said, looking out the window. "We'll go and get him after dark. But we'll need something to take care of that lock."

"I'll tear it open," Cain said.

"I know you're strong, but a padlock?"

Cain grinned. "Don't worry, my friend."

When Dunn and Sands entered Brock Clement's house, their host was sitting at the dining room table, having dinner.

"Just in time, gents," he said. "Pull up a chair and have something to eat."

"Hey, great—" Sands started.

"After you clean up, that is," Clement added with a grin on his handsome face.

Dunn grinned back.

"Yeah, okay." He looked at Sands. "Let's get cleaned up."

                          *   *   *

When they returned to the dining room, there were two other
places set at the table. Dunn and Sands sat across from each
other, with Clement at the head of the table.

"Help yourselves, boys," their host said.

There were platters on the table with fried chicken, vegetables, and fresh biscuits.

"You eat like this all the time?" Sands asked, jabbing a
huge chicken breast with his fork and transferring it to his
plate.

"Oh yes," Clement said, "all the time."

"You're a young fella," Sands said. "How'd you get so
much money so young?"

"I'm thirty-five," Clement said. "I just look younger.
Some of the money I inherited, some of it I made myself."

"That's enough, Sands," Dunn said. "Brock is our host.
He doesn't have to answer so many questions."

"May I ask some?" Clement said.

"Sure." Dunn speared a chicken leg, filled his plate with
vegetables.

"Is the Gunsmith in town yet?"

"We don't know," Dunn said. "We haven't seen him, so
we're gonna need your help findin' out."

"How can I help?"

"Send some of your people into town to have a look
around," Dunn said with his mouth full. "Hotels, saloons.
See if they spot the Gunsmith."

"I'll need a description."

"I'll give you one after dinner."

Clement took a deep breath.

"You know," he said to Dunn, "when you saved my life,
I knew I'd be in your debt, but somehow I thought you were
going to ask for money."

"If I had asked for money, would you have gave it to me?"
Dunn asked.

"Of course."

Dunn looked at Sands, who shrugged, wondering why Dunn had not asked for money. He would have if he'd had a rich man in his debt.

"Well," Dunn said, "maybe later. Right now we just need a place to stay, and some help."

"And what about the horse in my carriage house?"

"What the hell is a carriage house anyway?" Sands asked. Clement looked at him.

"Usually a place where you keep a carriage. That's why I have one in there."

Sands fell silent, feeling like he'd been told he was stupid. He wouldn't have taken it, except that they were Clement's guests, he was helping them, so Sands had to keep his mouth shut.

"We'll just keep the horse there," Dunn said, "but I think in the morning we should start putting a man in there with him."

"Tell them to keep clear," Sands said, holding up his bandaged hand.

"I'll remind them," Clement said. He looked at Dunn. "After this, we are even, Adam?"

"Even, Brock," Dunn said.

"Good," Clement said. "I don't want to have to worry about you constantly showing up."

Dunn put his silverware down with a loud clang.

"Have I asked you for anythin' before this?"

"No, but—"

"So stop complainin', Brock," Dunn said. "This is the one and only time you'll see me, and I don't need any of your money."

"Yes, all right," Clement said. "Forgive me, Adam. I meant no offense."

Dunn picked up his utensils and went back to the meal.

THIRTY-NINE

Clint and Cain moved through the darkness, skirting the house so as not to be caught in any of the light coming from the windows.

"They don't have anybody on watch?" Cain asked.

"Not that I could see this afternoon," Clint said. "We have to do this before that changes, though."

"I am going to be very interested in the motive behind all of this," Cain admitted.

"So am I," Clint said. Although, since it had been happening more and more lately, he thought that it might just be a case of his past popping up to bite him on the ass . . . again!

They reached the carriage house and Cain saw the lock on the front doors.

"Is there a back door?" he asked.

"Let's look."

They went by the window Clint had looked in earlier in the day. It was pitch black inside, so they couldn't see anything. Clint hoped his trusted Darley Arabian was still inside.

They got around to the back, found another pair of double doors similarly locked with a padlock. This one, however, seemed a bit flimsier, and a little rusted.

"Ah," Cain said. He took out his knife and, using the blade and his brute strength, snapped the lock in no time, with almost no noise.

They opened the doors slowly, just in case the hinges creaked, but there was no danger of that. They paused in the doorway to let their eyes adjust to the darkness. The first thing they saw was the carriage in the center of the room. Movement off to one side drew their eyes, and there was Eclipse, staring balefully at Clint as if asking, "What took you so long?"

"Hey, big fella," Clint whispered.

"What?" Cain said.

"Not you," Clint said, "him."

Clint walked to Eclipse and patted his neck and nose, then untied the reins that were holding him.

"What now?" Cain asked.

"Let's get him out of here," Clint said. "Once we get him somewhere safe, we're in a much better position in any showdown."

"Let's get out of here, then."

They walked the big horse out the back door, then had to decide which way to go. Should they take the chance of walking him right by the house?

"Let's circle around back here," Clint suggested. "Then we can walk him by one of the other houses to get to the road."

"Agreed," Cain said.

That's what they did. They walked the horse across several backyards, then turned and walked him to the road, going by a house that was completely dark. Just when they thought they were home free, though, a light went on in front of the house and a voice called out, "Who's out there?"

They turned and saw an old woman standing on the porch. She was wearing a cotton housedress, and holding an old but mean-looking shotgun.

"Just walking my horse, ma'am," Clint said to her.

"In my yard, young man?" she said. "What do you take me for? Who's that with you?"

"Just my friend."

"He's a big one," she said.

"My friend, or my horse?" Clint asked.

"Both."

"Ma'am," Cain said, "we were just walking by."

She squinted at them.

"A couple of these houses have been robbed lately," she told them.

"That's terrible, ma'am," Clint said, "but I assure you, we're not robbers. We were just walking."

"Uh-huh," she said. "Well, I'll be talking to the sheriff in the morning."

"That's fine, ma'am," Clint said. "You do that."

She gestured with the shotgun barrel and said, "Now get the hell off my property."

"Yes, ma'am," Clint said. "Our pleasure."

He led Eclipse out of the woman's yard and onto the street, followed by Cain, who was waiting to hear the old woman cock her shotgun.

The sound never came.

FORTY

They picked up their other horses from in front and in back of the hotel then walked all three to a livery stable. They had to knock on the doors to get in, but soon enough a man swung them open and said, "It's the middle of the night."

"We've got three horses for you to take care of," Clint said, "and we'll pay double."

The man swung the doors wide open and said, "Come on in, then. Wow, that's a big one."

Clint had decided not to take the horses to the livery where old Jake worked. He just didn't have any confidence in the old drunk to take proper care of them. This man was younger, though by no means a youngster. At least he was sober.

They waited while the man took all three horses to their stalls, then when he came back, Clint handed him some money.

"How long?" the man asked, looking at the money in his hand.

"Hopefully," Clint said, "one day."

"This is more than double, then."

"Keep it," Clint said. "Take real good care of them, especially the big one."

"You bet," the man said.

"And if anyone else knocks tonight," Clint said, "don't answer the door."

"Fine with me," the man said. "I was asleep anyway."

They left, waited for the man to close the double doors and lock them before moving off.

"Check on the horse," Dunn told Sands.

"Again?"

"Just do it!"

Sands got up from the table and left the room.

Clement poured himself some more wine.

"When do you think this little matter will wrap up?" he asked Dunn.

"I hope tomorrow," Dunn said.

"Is he reliable?" Clement asked, jerking his chin toward Sands's vacated chair.

"Reliable enough."

"We haven't talked about it, but this is a job, right?" Clement asked. "Not something personal?"

"It started out as a job," Dunn said. "It's still somethin' I'm gettin' paid for, but now it's become personal."

"Because it's been so difficult to kill him?"

Dunn nodded.

"A man like that, I suppose he's been through this many times," Clement said.

"Well," Dunn said, "I hope this'll be the last time."

Just at the moment Dunn spoke, Sands came running in from the back door.

"He's gone!"

"What?"

"The horse is gone," Sands said. "The back door is open. The lock's broke."

"That rear lock was kind of rusty," Clement admitted. "Maybe the horse kicked the door?"

"Maybe," Dunn said, standing up, "or maybe somebody came and got 'im. Come on, let's look around."

He and Sands went out the back door.

Clint suggested they stop at a saloon.

"Why?" Cain asked. "Let's just go back to the house."

"Come on," Clint said, "I'll tell you my thinking over a beer."

"Well, I could use a beer," the big half-breed said. In fact, he'd been feeling that way ever since he left the whorehouse.

They stopped in the first saloon they came to. It was well lit, half full, probably because it offered no gambling. There was only one girl working the floor, and she looked exhausted. There were three men at the bar. Clint and Cain took up a position at a far end, where they wouldn't be over-heard.

"Two beers," Clint said, waving at the bored-looking bartender. The man reacted immediately and set two full mugs in front of them.

"Okay," Cain said after drinking half his beer down gratefully, "what is on your mind?"

"I'm wondering what they will do when they discover Eclipse missing. That lock was rusty. They might just think he kicked the door open."

"Or," Cain said, "they'll think you were here."

"Right."

"Might make them nervous."

"Right again."

"So we stand here and nurse a couple of beers and let them sweat."

"My thinking exactly."

Dunn and Sands checked the floor in the carriage house, Dunn holding a lamp high.

"Footprints," he said, pointing.

"Could be ours," Sands said.

Dunn pointed down.

"That's a big man's foot."

"Not the Gunsmith's?"

"I doubt it," Dunn said, "but there are two sets here."

"Then he's here," Sands said, "and he has help. And we don't have his horse anymore."

Dunn moved the lamp, looked at the broken lock, then checked the door.

"No chance the horse kicked it open?"

"There's always a chance," Dunn said. "Come on, let's follow these tracks."

Using the lamp, they followed the tracks. It was helpful that the horse's tracks were so big, as were those made by one of the men. Even in the lamplight, they were able to follow.

They were walking by a darkened house toward the main road when a light came on and a voice called out.

"Stand still!"

They stopped, looked up onto the porch at the old woman holding a shotgun.

"Goddamnit!" she said. "Too many damn people walkin' around in the dark tonight." She squinted. "You ain't the same men."

"Which men, ma'am?" Dunn asked.

"Why should I answer your questions?"

"Well, we're guests of one of your neighbors, Mr. Clement," Dunn said.

"I know Clement," she said. "Don't like him."

"His house was robbed, and we're tryin' to figure out who did it."

"Robbed, huh?" she said. "They tol' me they wasn't robbers."

"Who told you that, ma'am?"

"Them men with the horse."

Dunn looked at Sands.

"Can you describe them?" Dunn asked.

"Only one. He was a big fella. And the horse. He was a big one, too."

"Do you know where they went?"

"I don't know," she said, "and I don't give a damn. I tol' them to get off my land, and I'm tellin' you the same thing."

"Yes, ma'am," Dunn said. "Thanks for your help."

They walked to the road, at which time she went back inside and the light went out.

"Let's get back to Clement's house," Dunn said. They began to walk along the road.

"She didn't describe Adams," Sands said.

"She couldn't describe the second man," Dunn said. "It was him, all right. Goddamn, I really wanna kill him!"

"We're gonna need help."

"We've got it."

"Your friend Clement?" Sands asked. "He's gonna help us kill a man?"

"He owes me big," Dunn said.

"Yeah, about that," Sands said. "You never did tell me the whole story."

"That's right," Dunn said. "I never did."

He didn't say anything else after that, so they continued on to the Clement house in silence.

FORTY-ONE

Inside, Clement was having coffee.

"So?"

"Looks like Adams came for the horse, and had some help," Dunn said. He walked to the table, poured himself some coffee. "We're gonna need your help, Brock."

"I have been helping you."

"We're gonna need men."

"To help you kill the Gunsmith?"

Dunn nodded. Sands poured himself some coffee, drank it nervously.

"Don't tell me a man with your money ain't never had anybody killed," Dunn said.

Clement wiped his mouth with a napkin and looked at Dunn.

"If I have ever done that, I had good reason," their host said. "To do it again, I'd need a good reason."

"You know the reason," Dunn said. "It would square us."

"Square us," Clement said.

Dunn nodded.

Clement pushed his chair back.

"Why don't we go into the den," he said, "and have some brandy."

"Ain't got any whiskey?" Sands asked.

"Brandy's fine," Dunn said, giving Sands a hard look. "Let's have some brandy."

They followed their host into the den, where he poured. The only other person in the house was the cook. Everything else Clement did for himself.

"Dunn, you'll have your men tomorrow morning."

"Are they good with guns?"

"They can use them."

"Will they do what I tell them?"

"If I tell them to."

"And if you pay them enough, right?" Sands asked.

"Actually," Clement said, "that is correct."

"How will you get word to them?" Dunn asked.

"Don't you worry about that," Clement said. "They'll be here tomorrow."

Dunn and Sands exchanged a glance.

"All right," Dunn said. "We'll wait 'til mornin', then."

"And do what until then?" Sands asked.

"Just relax."

"You mind if I worry a little?"

"No," Dunn said, standing up, "but it'll keep you awake."

"That's for sure," Clement said. "I learned a long time to leave my worrying outside my bedroom."

"You got money," Sands said. "Makes it easy."

"Money just brings worry, Mr. Sands," Clement said. "And more money brings more worries."

"Well, I'd like to try me some of them worries sometime," Sands said.

"When do you want to go?" Cain asked Clint. They were working on their second beers.

"I've been thinking about that."

"What have you come up with?"

"I'm wondering how worried they'll be by morning. Worried men are careless."

"On the other hand," Cain said, "if they do not discover that the horse is missing until morning, they will not have spent the night worrying."

"Good point," Clint said, "but I had another thought."

"What's that?"

"I've been tracking these two men a long time," Clint said. "I'd like to see them in the daylight."

"Between now and then they might get some help."

"I'm tired of this," Clint said. "I'll face however many men they want to throw at me. You don't have to come along."

"I have come this far," Cain said. "I will go the rest of the way with you."

"You'll need a shotgun, then," Clint said, "for close-up work. We can get one in the morning."

"I won't argue with that."

"Drink up, then," Clint said. "We better turn in. We got a busy morning ahead of us."

Cain nodded, and drank.

"One more thing," Clint said.

"What's that?"

"What really happened with you in that whorehouse?"

FORTY-TWO

In the morning when Dunn came down from his second-floor bedroom, there were four men sitting in the living room. In the dining room Clement was eating breakfast. Sands had not yet come down.

"These your best men?" Dunn asked.

"Yes."

"Have they had breakfast?"

"I don't know."

"You mean you ain't fed them?"

"I said they'd be here for your use," Clement said, "I said nothing about feeding them. Go and have your breakfast. Where is Mr. Sands?"

"He'll be down." Dunn sat, took some eggs, ham, and biscuits. If Clement wasn't worried about feeding the men, why should he be?

Sands came down minutes later and joined them.

"Them the men?" he asked.

"They are," Dunn said.

"Don't look like much."

"They can shoot," Clement said, "and they will not run when the action begins."

"You seem to know what's important with men like this," Dunn said.

Clement didn't comment.

"We ain't talked about your business," Dunn said.

"That's because it's my business," Clement said.

"Yeah, okay."

They ate.

Clint met Cain in the lobby and they went to a café for breakfast. Over steak and eggs they spoke of their day.

"You want to wait for them to come for us?" Cain asked.

"No," Clint said, "I want to call the play."

"So we just walk up to the house?"

"Yep."

"No matter how many of them there are?" Cain asked.

Clint nodded.

"Why?"

"It'll unnerve them," Clint said, "especially if there's five or more. They won't expect us to stand against those odds."

"I wouldn't expect to either."

"We can ambush them if you want."

Cain shook his head.

"Not your way, or mine," Cain said. "We'll face 'em head-on. Unnerve 'em."

"Yes."

Cain waved for the waiter.

"If I am to die today, I want another steak."

It sounded like a good idea to Clint.

After breakfast Dunn and Sands faced the four men. As they entered the living room, the men stood up.

"Mr. Clement tell you why I wanted you?" Dunn asked.

"No," one of them said. "He said you'd do that."

"We've been hired to kill somebody," Dunn said. "Anybody here got trouble killin' for money?"

The four men all shook their heads, while one—who seemed to be the spokesman—said, "No."

"Good."

"When do we do this?" the man asked.

"With any luck, this morning."

"Who's the man?"

Dunn studied the four men, then asked, "Is that important? You're gettin' paid."

"Just curious."

"His name's Clint Adams," Dunn said. He watched for reactions. "Anybody wanna back out?"

The four men didn't react.

"No," the spokesman said. "We're in."

"The Gunsmith is past his time," one of the others said.

Dunn looked at him. He was probably all of twenty-four.

"That so?"

"Old," the young man said. "He won't be no trouble."

Dunn didn't bother telling the boy how many men Adams had killed recently, how many he and Sands had already sent against him.

"Maybe," Dunn said.

"We goin' out lookin' for him?" the spokesman asked.

Dunn looked at Sands, then back at the men.

"No," Dunn said, "he knows where we are. He'll come here."

"Today," Sands said.

"We best get set up to receive him," Dunn said. "Oh, one more thing."

"What's that?" the spokesman asked.

"He won't be alone."

"How many?"

"Just one more."

"No problem," the young man said.

Dunn was willing to bet that this jasper would be the first one killed.

* * *

Clint and Cain finished their breakfast and left the café. They stopped in front and checked the street. It would have been easy if Dunn, Sands, and whoever else they recruited were waiting there for them.

"What about the sheriff?" Cain asked.

"We'll deal with him after the fact," Clint said.

"If we're alive."

"There is that."

FORTY-THREE

Clint approached the house alone.

The front door opened and a man stepped out, followed by a second.

"Adams?" the man asked.

"That's right," Clint said. "Which one are you, Dunn or Sands?"

Dunn looked mildly surprised that Clint had managed to come up with their names.

"I'm Dunn, he's Sands."

"What's this been about, Dunn?" Clint asked.

Dunn shrugged.

"Just a job."

"Really? For money? All this has been for money?"

"Started out that way," Dunn said. "Got kind of personal when you started killing my men."

"Got personal for me when you tried to bushwhack me," Clint said. "Even more when you stole my horse."

"Well," Dunn said, "you got him back, unharmed."

"Somehow," Clint said, "that doesn't settle things."

Suddenly, a third man came out the door, unarmed, dressed well. Clint figured he was the owner of the house.

"Gentlemen," he said, "can we take this activity away from my house?"

"Afraid not, friend," Clint said. "You opened your house to these . . . gents . . . and you're going to have to deal with the consequences."

"Truly, sir," the man said, "there has been nothing personal in this for me. Except to repay my debt to Mr. Dunn for saving my life during a stagecoach robbery."

"I'm not concerned with your debt to Mr. Dunn," Clint said, "only mine."

Clement looked dismayed, but had no answer for that.

"Where's the rest of your crew, Dunn?" Clint asked.

"The rest?"

"If I've learned anything about you, it's that you always have backup. Men you're willing to give up if you have to."

"And you?" Dunn said. "According to the tracks you left when you got your horse back, you've got a man with you."

"Just for true backup," Clint said. "So I don't get bushwhacked again."

"Well," Dunn said, "that was a mistake. This time it's between you and us."

"And these two," a voice said to Clint's right.

He, Dunn, Sands, and Clement all looked and saw Cain holding a man in each hand by their collar. The men seemed unconscious as he dropped them to the ground.

"And I will bet there are two on the other side of the house," Cain said.

At that point the two he was referring to stepped out and started shooting.

"No!" Clement shouted. "Wait!"

The others had no choice.

Dunn and Sands drew their guns.

Clint cleared leather well before they did.

Cain went into a crouch and raised his rifle. However, for a man almost seven feet tall, a crouch looked like a normal standing man. He made an impressive target, and the men from the other side of the house forgot their instructions to focus on Clint and began to fire at the big half-breed.

Dunn noticed quickly that the young man he had assumed would die first was now firing at the half-breed. The Indian fired back, and shot the young man in the chest.

First one dead, as he'd predicted.

Unless the two at the Indian's feet were also dead.

He drew his gun, and saw that Clint Adams's gun was already out.

Damn, he thought, not so past it.

As the lead began to fly, Clement hit the deck and covered his head with both hands, still yelling "Stop! Stop! Stop!" The lead slammed into the wall of his house, and broke the glass in the front window, showering him with fragments.

He was beginning to be sorry Adam Dunn had ever saved his life.

Then he heard other sounds, wet, slapping ones as lead struck flesh, and he felt the warmth of blood on him.

Someone else's blood.

Clint fired quickly, taking Dunn in the belly and Sands in the chest and head. He saw the blood fly from Sands's head.

He looked over at Cain, who was down on one knee firing his rifle. Suddenly, the big man jerked and Clint knew he'd been hit.

He turned his attention to the two men who were firing at Cain. The big half-breed was right. He wasn't that good with a rifle. One of them was down, but one was still firing. Clint squeezed off a quick shot and put him down.

And it was quiet . . . except for Clement, who was still screaming, this time because somebody's blood was on him, and he thought it was his.

Clint went to check on Cain first . . .

"You hit?" he asked.

The big man was still down on one knee and said, "Clipped me on the hip."

"Bad?"

"It is . . . numb."

"Okay," Clint said, "lie back."

Instead, Cain got to his feet.

"Let's see if we can stop that man from screaming," he said.

Clint went to the porch, with Cain limping behind him. He leaned over Clement and checked him out.

"Okay, you're all right," he said, "stop screaming, stop—" He slapped the man in the face, which cut off the screaming right away.

"Stand up," he said, putting his hand beneath the man's arm. "You're all right. It's not your blood."

"It's—it's not?"

"No," Clint said. He helped the man to a chair on the porch and said, "Sit."

Clement sat, patting himself to see if Clint was right.

"This one is still alive," Cain said, "but not for long."

Clint walked over, looked at Dunn. Cain was right. The man was gut-shot, and all color had drained from his face. His eyes were dull, but they were open.

Clint leaned over the dying man.

"Dunn, who hired you?" he asked. "Who hired you to kill me?"

Dunn laughed, but it sounded like a death rattle.

"You better . . . start watching . . . your back trail . . . really close . . . he's got a lot of money . . . a lot of . . ."

The man died.

Clint stood up, looked at Cain, whose face was stoic, but etched in pain.

"Come on," he said, "let's get you to a doctor."

FORTY-FOUR

Her nipples were so hard he could feel them through her blouse. When she reached back to feel between his legs, she found that he was hard as well. Clint pulled her blouse loose so he could reach beneath it to fondle her bare breasts. Her breaths were quick and shallow. When he started pulling her skirts up around her waist, she groaned, "Yes. God, yes."

Clint unbuckled his belt and couldn't get his pants down quick enough. Once they were out of his way, he tore off the last of Maria's undergarments and hiked her skirts all the way up. As soon as she felt his hand on the small of her back, she leaned forward and grabbed on to the table in front of her as if she'd been shoved down. Judging by the way she moaned Clint's name and spread her legs apart for him, she wouldn't have protested one bit if he had taken an even stronger hand with her.

Maria's ass was round and firm in front of him. Clint took a moment to admire her curves, but couldn't wait long before guiding his rigid pole into her. She let out a slow, shuddering breath as Clint gripped her hips tightly, pulled her close, and buried his cock as far in as it would go. Just when it seemed she was about to burst with anticipation, he began pumping in and out.

At first, Maria let him go at his own pace. Soon, however, she started bucking against him, prompting him to pound into her even harder. Every impact rolled through her body to rattle the table against the floor. Whipping her hair back, she grunted, "Yes! Fuck me harder."

Clint reached forward to put one hand on her shoulder while keeping the other on her ass. Every time he pumped into her, he shook her entire body. Maria groaned loudly, slapping the table with one hand while moaning, "Harder!"

Now Clint put both hands on her shoulders and pulled her toward him with every thrust. Every now and again, he caught a glimpse of a smile on her face when she craned her neck to look back at him while letting out a breathy grunt.

Clint reached around to feel her breasts swaying with the motion of his body pounding into hers, and then settled both hands once again on her plump buttocks. She was so wet between her legs that he glided in and out of her with ease. As much as she'd demanded for him to speed up, he drove her even wilder when he slowed down.

Holding her in place, he eased back until he was almost out of her and then slid back in so he could feel her lips glide over every inch of him. Maria arched her back and clawed at the table. When he moved back and forth in the same manner, she trembled with an approaching climax. Then, after sliding out again, Clint drove into her with everything he had and kept thrusting until she screamed loud enough to be heard in the next county.

Maria's voice was breathless when she tried to say his name, which didn't stop Clint from pumping into her again and again. When he finally exploded inside her, she was too winded to say much of anything at all . . .

Clint had returned to Hastings with Cain, making sure the half-breed got back safely. He'd driven him there in a buckboard, with their horses trailing along behind.

However, before leaving Kerrville, he had stopped in to see Clement again.

"It was impossible to get the blood off my clothes," the man said, letting him in. "I had to burn them."

"You're lucky that's all you had to do," Clint said. "I could press charges against you, you know."

"For what?" Clement seemed shocked.

"You gave them a place to stay, hid my horse even though you knew it was stolen, and supplied them with men to kill me."

"I didn't . . . they threatened me. I was in fear of my life."

"Never mind the lies," Clint said. "If I pressed charges, I'd have to stay around here."

"So you're not?"

"No," Clint said, "but I have one last question."

"What is it?"

"Was it you?"

"Was what me?" Clement asked, looking genuinely confused.

"Was it you who hired them to kill me?"

"God, no! Why would I do that?"

"Before he died, Dunn said the man who hired him had a lot of money," Clint said.

"That doesn't mean it was me."

"I could kill you right now, just to make sure."

Clement moved back a few steps, put his hands up in front of his face, and said, "You—you can't!"

"I can," Clint said, "but I won't. But if I find out it was you, I'll be back, and I will kill you."

"It—it wasn't me. I swear!"

Clint left the house, feeling fairly sure Clement wasn't the man behind Dunn and Sands.

But who was?

Clint left Maria asleep in the room, checked out of his hotel, and walked outside to where Eclipse was waiting.

"Sorry, big fella," he said, rubbing the Darley Arabian's nose, "this one got a little out of hand."

He mounted up and rode out of Hastings. This wasn't over. There was still a man out there—a man with many resources—who wanted him dead.

Not over at all.

Watch for

MEXICO MAYHEM

387th novel in the exciting GUNSMITH series
from Jove

Coming in March!

GIANT ACTION! GIANT ADVENTURE!

THE GUNSMITH

J.R. ROBERTS

penguin.com/actionwesterns

M455AS0812